The LIST of REAL THINGS

SARAH MOORE FITZGERALD

Orion
Children's B

ORION CHILDREN'S BOOKS

First published in Great Britain in 2018 by Orion Children's Books

1 3 5 7 9 10 8 6 4 2

Text copyright © Sarah Moore Fitzgerald, 2018

The moral rights of the author have been asserted.

A CIP catalogue record for this book
is available from the British Library.

ISBN: 978 1 4440 1481 5

Printed and bound in Great Britain by
Clays Ltd, St Ives plc

The paper and board used in this book are
made from wood from responsible sources.

Orion Children's Books

An imprint of
Hachette Children's Group
Part of Hodder and Stoughton
Carmelite House
50 Victoria Embankment
London EC4Y 0DZ

An Hachette UK Company

www.hachette.co.uk
www.hachettechildrens.co.uk

For Eoghan, Stef and Gabbie

PROLOGUE

If there was ever a building somewhere on the tall cliffs behind Dillon's Park, as some people say there once was, then it's probably not there any more. My grandfather told me it was only a rumour, started long ago – a story that parents used to tell their children to frighten them into staying away from the dangerous heights above the beach.

Hotel Magnificent is what they used to call it – a place that was said to be full of ghosts who could be heard singing and calling out, and would pull you up into it if you got too close.

There's no proof anywhere that a place like that existed. The cliff path is broken and inaccessible now, so even if you were curious and wanted to go and see for yourself, there's no way up any more.

Most people say there isn't anything to be scared of around Dillon's Park and that there's nothing weird or ghostly about its surroundings.

Personally, I'm glad the old story has more or less died out. It's hard enough to pay proper attention to all the things in this life that are actually real without being distracted by things that are not.

ONE

B ee claimed that the faces of our parents were clear inside her head, but there was no possible way she was telling the truth. I could barely picture them myself, and I'm five years older than her. I tried hard to remind myself of the sounds of their voices, the words they could have spoken, the songs they might have sung. But it was like opening my eyes under water, or squinting through thick fog at something far away. I could only ever make out the haziest of smudgy shapes, the vaguest of muffled sounds.

I didn't like to dwell on what had happened to them. Whenever Bee asked me about it, all I would say was that one morning, when she was small, our mum had died. And then, not long after that, so had our dad. It was a relief that she didn't look for more details, and unusual too, considering how curious she normally was.

Uncle Freddy had been travelling around the world when the news reached him and there was nothing to do but come straight home because Bee and I were there, bewildered and sad and waiting for someone to take care of us. The captains of our lives were gone and so was the great safe boat of love that we'd sailed in. It felt as if we were very small, like tiny corks bobbing around and lost in a frightening sea.

It was Uncle Freddy who rescued us. In the shock and sorrow of our sudden parentlessness, I wasn't too sure what we would have done without him, or where we would have gone, or how we might have felt.

'It makes one shudder to think!' as Bee often said.

Uncle Freddy had long hair and tanned skin with little fans of white lines around his eyes where the sun hadn't reached because of all the smiling. If his Facebook page was anything to go by, before he became our guardian he'd spent a huge amount of time on boats in hot places, on water that glittered and flashed all around him like a diamond-scattered blue blanket.

We loved Uncle Freddy instantly. He hardly ever got cross, and when he did, we always had plenty of warning because of a deep crease that crumpled on the bridge of his nose.

The first thing he did when he arrived was fix the windows in the living room, and the kitchen, and the hall, which had all somehow got broken – I didn't remember how.

He bought a big pack of modelling clay and made strange small heads with massive nostrils and frowning faces and he built a shelf on the outside of our bedroom door where we put those little statues. 'These are gargoyles,' he told us.

'Why are they so ugly?' I asked.

'They have to be like that,' he replied, smiling and ruffling my hair, 'otherwise they wouldn't be any good. They're there to protect you. They ward off evil spirits.'

After that Bee got into a habit of marching around the house saying, 'Gargoyles,' over and over again.

Uncle Freddy rearranged the kitchen and bought us whatever we wanted to eat and I remember telling him that Bee liked sweets even though at that point she'd never eaten or asked for a sweet in her life.

Best of all, Uncle Freddy arranged for our Grandfather Patrick to move out of his nursing home so he could come to live with us too.

'Hello, girls!' said our grandfather in the doorway, leaning on a silver-tipped walking stick, his lovely shadow darkening the hall. 'I'm delighted to be here! And it's wonderful of you to have me. I do hope you won't find me a nuisance.'

As soon as she saw him, Bee reached out for him with her soft-creased toddler hands.

Granddad Patrick was stronger than he looked. He

gathered both of us up into a hug. It felt a bit clumsy and I was kind of embarrassed, but Bee leaned her head against Granddad's chest, and that was more or less it. Kindred spirits from that moment on. No separating them.

It would have been lovely to stay in that big, warm, happy hug for longer, but there were bags to be carried in and belongings to be unpacked.

It was only when I was dragging Granddad's suitcase through the door that I noticed the basket on the ground, and in it, a messy little curled-up clump of wool, moving slightly.

'What's this?'

'I thought you'd never ask!' he said. 'You can pick him up if you'd like.'

I crouched down closer to the bundle, which had ears that twitched and eyes that turned towards me.

'Airedale Terrier,' said Granddad.

'What?'

'He'll grow big, but right now he's only little, just like Bee.' Bee squeaked and then held on to the dog's ears, squeezing them with a weird kind of seriousness that made me worried, but from the very start, that dog never minded what she did. He seemed totally fine as she kept on squishing him, happy even. And he looked into her eyes with nothing but hope.

'Is he ours?' I had asked.

'Yes.'

6

'Really?'

'Yes, really. His name's Louie.'

I didn't care what he was called. He needed us, and we needed him, and that was that.

As soon as Granddad moved in, we got to know Janine too. She came to the house three times a week. She had sparkly nails and lovely shoes and dark red lipstick that made Bee stare.

'It's very nice to meet you,' she'd said on her first visit, shaking my hand and rubbing Bee's plump little cheek with her finger.

Janine's long-term plan was to open up a nail and beauty bar, but right now her job was to mind Granddad because even though he was strong and wilful he was old too. Very old. And he needed help with certain things like shaving and figuring out which pills to take when. She always brought presents, including a bright pink pill box for Granddad with compartments for each day of the week.

'I'm your granddad's carer,' she told us, smiling and handing us cardboard tubes full of chocolate chips.

'It's a disguise!' Granddad said. 'She's really my secret girlfriend.'

Janine rolled her eyes.

On Granddad's poker nights, Janine helped us out by preparing massive piles of sandwiches and baking cakes.

'It's not strictly in my job description,' she told us, 'but he does love his cards.'

She got to know all his friends, especially Lal and Gertie. 'Demons of the game,' Granddad called them. Scully, my only friend at the time, usually came along too. Janine wasn't sure if it was appropriate for us to be gambling with what she liked referring to as 'the old sharks'.

'Nonsense!' Granddad would say. 'They lower the average age at this table by a very welcome amount. And besides, won't they keep us on our toes?' The old sharks were already on their toes as far as we could see.

Scully and I would sit ready for the deal, and Granddad and Lal and Gertie would grin at us saying oblique things like 'always double when everyone checks,' and 'never bet into but always see a one card buy.'

We let Louie sleep anywhere, first in our room and then on our beds. We fed him from the table. 'No boundaries – that's the problem. He's spoiled rotten,' was what Uncle Freddy said, but his eyes were all shiny as usual, and I could see he wasn't really cross. He never got cross about anything that dog did.

Louie's wildness was his brilliance. It made him bark at strangers and it gave him the energy to run like a furry bullet up and down the rocks by Dillon's Park, growling at the sea.

*

I used to watch other people's mothers at the school gates, and listen to what they said, and I tried to say the same kind of things to Bee, just to make sure she didn't lose out on anything.

'Do you have your lunchbox?'

'Brush your hair!'

'Mind the step!'

'Watch for cars!'

Things like that.

And then, slowly, as time went by, I suppose we almost completely forgot about our parents.

'Sure, children are so adaptable,' Lal or Gertie often declared from the poker table. And everyone would nod their heads as the cards were dealt.

We loved those nights. It was fun to be part of them, pouring whiskey and making tea and serving sandwiches and huge slices of Janine's cakes for everyone.

Sometimes, Uncle Freddy's friends would put on their sad faces when they looked at us. 'Ah, Telpis,' they'd say.

'There's nothing tragic about these two,' Uncle Freddy would insist. 'It doesn't do to be defined by misfortune or heartbreak. Day-to-day life is hard enough without being haunted by the shadows of grief.'

I didn't really know what he meant but I knew he wanted us to be happy. So even though there were unnamed oceans of sadness deep and dark inside me, I did my best.

Before Bee was old enough to come with us, my granddad would take me fishing down by the shore. I learned to cast a spinner into the sea and reel it in, and I'd be full of expectation and hope that we would catch something as we talked. But the sea seemed empty in Dalkey Sound. They'd been over-fishing along the whole coast for years, and there was nothing left to be caught. In the end we stopped trying. Then one day Uncle Freddy went to the shed to look for something and he caught his finger on a fishhook. After that, the rods got thrown away, I think.

It wasn't until last summer that Bee came across this dented old Christmas card.

It had an extra fold right across the middle where there shouldn't have been one. She'd found it right at the bottom of an old, black wooden box that Uncle Freddy kept things in.

'*To my darling Grace and Beatrice,*' she read in a thin, slow, wobbly voice that made me ache. '*This card guarantees a camp night in Dillon's Park. Next summer, when Mum is better and Bee is a little older, and all this is over, the four of us will sleep in a tent. We will light a bonfire and look at the stars and stay until morning, and we'll fish with rods and spinners on the top of Seaweed Rock. Have patience, girls, if you can. There are better times to come. Love from Dad.*'

10

A wave of different things seemed to flow through Bee: 'Dillon's Park! In a tent! Under the stars!' She locked her hands together like she was saying a prayer. 'Oh, Gracie, can you imagine such a thing!' And she danced around the room.

'Calm down, Bee,' I said.

Then she sat on the bed, gazing down at the card on her lap, and she read those last words over and over again. *'There are better times to come. There are better times to come.'*

'Oh God, Bee, can you stop it, please?' I begged, with no effect.

When Uncle Freddy came in from work, Bee was full-on crying. 'Better times never came!' she shouted at him.

'Bee, what is wrong?' said Uncle Freddy before I had a chance to explain.

'They never took me camping in Dillon's Park! They never kept their promise.'

'What's this about? Where's this coming from?' he asked, and somehow it was me who was angry then.

I waved the old card in the air, and it flapped near his face, all limp and dead-looking itself.

'Why did you leave this lying around? It was so careless of you, Uncle Freddy! Look what's happened now,' I said, pointing at Bee.

Nothing would soothe her until Granddad appeared. Then the two of them sat squashed up together on the sofa, staring into the fire with Louie spread extravagantly over both their laps.

'What were their names again?' sniffed Bee.

'Barbara and Daniel,' Granddad replied dreamily as he stroked Louie's woolly fur.

'How old was I?'

'You were three,' Granddad Patrick whispered.

'And how did they—'

'OK, ENOUGH ABOUT ALL THAT,' Uncle Freddy interrupted a good bit more loudly than usual. 'What I mean is . . . Crikey, look at the time. Everyone must be starving. Come on, now.' He clapped his hands and insisted that Granddad, Louie and Bee snapped out of their reverie and came to the kitchen.

Uncle Freddy cracked eggs into a bowl in a sudden fit of action. 'Girls – plates, glasses, salt, pepper,' he said as if laying the table had become the most urgent thing ever.

Maybe we'd been wrong. Maybe the card had been a chance, a message from the past, containing the voices and hints of our parents that had been buried in Uncle Freddy's box of stuff. Perhaps this had been an opportunity to talk to Bee about them. But the moment had gone.

It would have been hard to keep talking anyway because of the loud, busy *click-splash* of Uncle Freddy's whisking, filling everywhere with noise.

*

Bee didn't forget though. The Christmas card had planted an idea in her brain that wouldn't go away. And every day after that, the idea grew a little bit.

'What do you imagine it might be like to sleep in a tent?'

'I've no idea.'

'And what do the stars look like from Dillon's Park?'

'Dunno.'

'Do you think there's any chance we might still go camping there? Even though Mum and Dad can't take us?'

'Bee, I don't know,' I said.

'Uncle Freddy's a great fisherman. He used to camp all the time.'

'How do you know?'

'Grandfather Patrick told me. So maybe Uncle Freddy can take us.'

'Maybe,' I said.

'Should I ask him?'

'Do what you like.'

'OK, great, I will.'

Later, when we were walking home from school, Bee turned right at the end of Castle Street.

'Em, Bee, where do you think you're going?'

'To Uncle Freddy in the garage to ask him about the camping.'

'You can't go on your own.'

13

'You told me I could do what I liked.'

'OK, well, what I meant was to wait until he gets back from work. You can talk to him about it then.'

'Righto, jolly good,' she replied, skipping along beside me again.

As soon as we got in the door, she lugged a kitchen chair into the hall. She and Louie sat waiting and I just left her alone because sometimes there was no point in doing anything else.

When the key clicked in the door, Louie bounced and jumped and barked so crazily that I thought something was wrong. But it was just Uncle Freddy, holding his hands in the air and saying, 'Whoa, cool it, everyone. What's the problem?'

And Bee was all up in his face, telling him.

'I can't stop thinking about it! I simply cannot stop! It's in my mind the whole time!'

'What is?'

'The card from Dad and the message that's been in there, waiting for me to find it.'

'It wasn't waiting for anything, Bee,' I said. 'It's just an old piece of paper stuffed into a box.'

'Oh but no, Gracie, it's so much more than that! It is magic. It is giving me thoughts. Thoughts of starry nights, and they are so clear I can feel our backs on the spongy grass in Dillon's Park. I can't think of anything now except fishing and lighting fires and sleeping outdoors in a tent until the morning. It was our parents' promise. It's terribly exciting really, when you think about it.'

'Yes, Bee, I know,' Uncle Freddy said. 'It sounds as if it would have been a lot of fun all right. It was something they wanted to do , and I know they would have if . . . well, you know . . . if things had been different. But they can't do it now.'

'Of course I know *that*. But, Uncle Freddy, *you're* here, aren't you?' And her eyes were very wide and she was looking into his face with a frightening sort of focus. '*You* could take us instead. Couldn't you?'

Uncle Freddy rubbed his face with both his hands and said nothing.

Things had changed since my parents had been alive and one of the things was that now there was a big sign in Dillon's Park that said 'STRICTLY NO CAMPING'.

'What sign?' Bee said, frowning.

'The huge one right at the entrance,' I told her, 'in gigantic red letters.'

'It's not allowed,' added Uncle Freddy. 'And anyway, there are no fish left. You'd never catch anything there now.'

'Oh dear,' said Bee. 'What are you saying?'

'We're just trying to tell you . . .'

'You mean, we can't do it?' Louie stood beside her, looking pathetic.

'Listen, there are lots of other ways to have an adventure,' Uncle Freddy explained. 'We'll make it up to you somehow.'

She spent ages trying to change his mind. In the end Uncle Freddy finally said, 'Bee, that's enough, OK?' and when Bee knew there was no more arguing or pleading to be done, she became chillingly silent.

Her face was grave and her shoulders were slumped and something in her eyes went flat.

'I think I'll just go to bed now,' she said, eventually, and we could hear the dejected little thuds of her footsteps as she walked slowly up the stairs.

'Do you think she'll be OK?' Uncle Freddy asked me, but I didn't want to talk about it, mainly because I knew Bee was probably lying on the carpet in our bedroom with her ear to the floor. She and I often listened there together. Through the floorboards, you could hear every word in the kitchen floating up into our room.

By the time I'd gone up to her I wanted to listen too, the mumbles of Granddad's and Uncle Freddy's voices buzzing from below.

'I'm so out of my depth,' said Uncle Freddy.

'Our poor uncle,' Bee said, apparently fully cheered up. 'I do declare he's under quite a lot of mental pressure.'

We could hear him pacing, his voice more worried and taut than it ever was when he spoke to us.

'How can we talk about it to them, Dad, without bringing it all back?'

'Perhaps a camping trip wouldn't be such a bad idea,' Granddad's gentle voice suggested.

'No!' Uncle Freddy replied. 'I don't think it would be right of me to try to keep the promise that Barbara and Daniel weren't able to. I'd get it wrong. They'd be disappointed. Even if it wasn't illegal, the reality would never live up to the dream. And it would only make them wish for something they can't have.'

'I think we can change his mind,' whispered Bee, smiling now, as if she'd never been sad.

'Shush, Bee,' I said, because Uncle Freddy hadn't finished.

'That label of sadness must not stick to them for the rest of their lives. I mean, they're both so full of joy. I can't have them thinking of themselves as . . .'

And then he spoke very low as if it wasn't the kind of word you could ever say fully out loud:

'*Orphans.*'

TWO

'Wow, joy?' I said, surprised. 'And orphans? I guess I'd never really thought of us like that.'

'Gracie, honestly,' Bee answered. 'It's perfectly obvious that Uncle Freddy was only joking. Everybody knows that orphans aren't real.'

'What do you mean, they're not real?'

'I mean, they only happen in fairy tales – like unicorns and leprechauns and other things that don't exist. That's just silly.'

Many facts evaded Bee, which was funny when I thought about it considering how many non-facts she believed in with a disturbing strength of faith, including ghosts that controlled the weather.

The next day, Uncle Freddy took us to this green and purple office full of soft chairs where there was a low table and big mugs full of blunt crayons. Bee spent the whole time messily colouring in the pages of a mindfulness book. She stopped everything and stood up as soon as this woman called Mary came into the room. She told us she was a 'Feelings Doctor' and seemed perfectly nice to me, but Bee stared at her very suspiciously and slinked along with her back to the wall.

Mary asked Bee what it felt like to live with Uncle Freddy and Grandfather Patrick, and Bee said, 'GREAT! WONDERFUL! FANTASTIC! BRILLIANT!' in a ridiculously loud voice. And then she asked Bee if she ever felt sad about the fact that we didn't have parents.

'You must have us confused with somebody else,' Bee replied.

'Why do you say that?' asked Mary.

'Because we do have parents,' Bee said and then spent ages explaining that just because you couldn't see somebody, it didn't mean they weren't there.

'If you could wish for one thing, what would it be?' she asked Bee. I worried immediately that we were on hazardous ground.

'A magical, star-filled night of fishing in Dillon's Park, with a tent and a bonfire and sleeping under canvas and hearing the birds and trees all around us,' Bee replied.

'That sounds lovely,' said Mary.

'So I keep telling everyone,' said Bee.

Personally, I thought Mary was easy to talk to. I told her about this habit that I used to have of studying other people's mothers. I asked if she thought this made me strange.

'Not strange.' She gazed into my eyes. 'Just very responsible. And very kind.'

It wasn't really kindness or responsibility, I explained. I was only doing what I could to make sure that Bee could be more like everyone else: ordinary, unremarkable, normal.

Mary seemed especially polite and nice to Uncle Freddy.

'Are there any photographs of your sister and her husband?'

'Yes, plenty,' said Uncle Freddy. 'I even got them printed once.'

'And where do you keep them?'

'In a biscuit tin.'

'And do you or the girls ever look at them?'

'Em, no,' he said.

In a low voice he explained that he didn't look at them at all. 'Listen, you see,' he stumbled over his words, coughing from time to time. 'There is one thing I hate to do more than anything in the world and that is anything – anything at all – that might . . . that might . . . upset them.'

'I understand. I really do,' said Mary, her eyes all liquidy and her face all focused. 'Talking about death and sadness is difficult for everyone, especially under the circumstances. But all the evidence suggests that it is almost definitely better than not saying anything at all.'

Uncle Freddy nodded his head and then shook his head and then stayed perfectly still for a while. Bee and I looked at him and we looked at each other and I realised possibly for the first time ever that Uncle Freddy was sad too – maybe even the saddest of all of us – and somehow realising that made me feel terrible. Bee felt it as well, I thought. At least she gave me the same look that she usually gave me when we'd both done something wrong.

After we got home, Uncle Freddy went straight to the garden shed. When he came out, he was carrying the stepladder. He stood it in the kitchen and climbed to reach into a cupboard that was so high up we'd never noticed it before. He pulled out a dusty tin, and we watched as he put it on the table.

'You can look at these together if you'd like,' he said, and he went off to do something else.

'This is the happiest day of my life,' said Bee. She said that almost every day. 'I know what's inside!' she claimed, and she blew the dust off the top and lifted the lid.

She raised them out as if they were fragile and precious things: tons and tons of photos of our parents and of us with them. Everyone smiling. Bee a really tiny little baby, but still looking and reaching and watching and wide-eyed, just like always.

All Mum's details came back to me then – the line where

her forehead and her hair met, and her earlobes and the smile that was a little bit crooked but perfect all the same, and the literal glimmer that shone out of her and the half-moons of her nails – nothing but perfectness.

There was one photo of me and my dad paddling – him with bare feet, holding my hands, the bottom of his jeans wet, and it seemed as if I was dancing, the water splashing up around our faces. That was a real moment that once happened, and I did my best to remember it in my head but I couldn't – none of the sounds that must have been there or the smells or the feel of the sand and stone and water or the touch of my dad's hands. Just a flat, still picture.

Bee and I took the biscuit tin up to our room and Uncle Freddy never mentioned it again.

That night, in half-sleep, I began to hear their voices – the velvet of my father's whisper, the happy drumroll of my mother's laugh, the warm honey of their singing – and I began to cry. Hot, silent tears. The cruelty of their absence became like a real breathing thing. There was a hole in our lives, all ripped and ragged and raw. How had we learned to become so good at tiptoeing around it, pretending it wasn't there?

'What ails thee, Gracie?' Bee said when she heard me breathing heavily – my heart thumping crazily as if there was something alive, trapped inside me.

'Nothing, nothing – just dreaming,' I mumbled.

'Gracie, come on, what is it? Are you scared?' she asked.

'No, no, I'm not,' I managed to say.

'You are not alone,' she finally whispered. Louie jumped up on to her bed and wriggled around beside her.

I didn't really feel like continuing the conversation or telling her what was going on inside my head. It wouldn't do for Bee to hear about other people's bleak dreams in the night – it would only encourage her.

'You can be scared and brave at the same time,' she went on, undeterred. 'You know, Gracie, it doesn't matter. What matters is how loudly you sing when all feels as if it is lost. That's what Grandfather always says.'

'I don't want to sing loudly,' I argued.

'And what matters is getting out of bed in the morning to face the world even when your heart is dark with sadness.'

'Bee, shut up.'

'OK, I'm just saying. These are actually words of comfort that would be good for you if you listened,' she sniffed. In the bed beside her, Louie's tail thumped in agreement.

I needed Louie just as much as Bee did. I wanted to have him close and bury my face in his warm fur, and sometimes he would let me. But even if he was on my bed when I went to sleep, he was always on Bee's when I woke up.

All the members of my family wished Scully would come over even more often than he did, so when he called in the next day, everyone was typically delighted. Granddad couldn't get enough of him. He'd already practically forced Scully to become an honorary member of our family as soon as he'd discovered what a brilliant poker player he was.

Scully was the only one who really understood my Bee-related worries. He and I often went for a walk on the beach mainly so I could complain about her. 'You've no idea what a liability she is. Even admitting she's my sister these days feels like a social hazard,' I confided.

'I know where you're coming from,' Scully said, 'but nobody can really deny their sister. That's never the right thing to do.'

'Agreed!' roared a small, strong voice from behind us. 'It violates the principles of sisterly loyalty!'

It was Bee. She and Louie had this silent way of running on the sand that no one could figure out.

'She's such a funny little thing, isn't she?' Uncle Freddy said later after Bee and Granddad had come home from their own really long walk and Scully had gone home.

'I guess,' I replied. 'If by funny you actually mean mental.'

Bee and Louie were sprawled out, asleep, snoring like pigs.

'Bee is gifted, Gracie. She's been sanctified with a kind of blessing.'

'Yeah, right.'

The random notions that stirred inside her head didn't seem like blessings to me.

24

Night-time was especially dangerous, as though it brought with it a powerful stick, poking at the silty riverbed of Bee's imagination, making strange blacknesses swirl up from the deep.

It was after the photos that her nightmares began. Her whole body would tremble and I would say, 'Bee, Bee, wake up, Bee,' and in her sleep her eyelids would flutter and little moans and whimpers turned into shouting and then she would do her scream – a noise so stark and jagged it could have probably ripped paint off the wall.

'God almighty, Bee, someone's going to call the police,' I'd say after I'd shaken her awake. Uncle Freddy must have always had his earphones in, because he never seemed to hear.

I'd brush her tangled hair from her eyes and Louie would rest his chin on the end of her bed.

'What is it, Bee?'

'It's the woman again. She's like a skeleton and she has a long finger that she points at me and she grins a crazy grin and her eyes are dark and sinking into her bony face and she has no hair and she's coming to get me.'

'Nobody is coming to get you, Bee. You're safe in your bed and I'm right here beside you. It's a dream.'

It would take me ages to talk her down from the great heights of her panic, and to slow her pounding heart.

'All right then, I believe I am feeling a good deal better,' she would say, eventually, but I knew it was only to make me happy. I never thought I'd really convinced her and she would hold on so tight to Louie that he would look worried too. And even though she'd settle back down again and let me turn off the light, I could still hear her breath, fast and frightened, rushing in and out.

One thing that Uncle Freddy was really good at was ignoring things – things that he didn't like talking about. It was frustrating talking to him about Bee: the way she acted, the way she spoke, the things she thought and the things she said.

Bee had a lot of symptoms. She believed in ghosts. She had crazy visions at night. She spoke in that strange old-fashioned way that most people couldn't understand.

'There's something wrong with her,' I said.

Uncle Freddy closed his eyes and rubbed his face and said, 'Please, Gracie. There is NOTHING wrong with your sister and you are to stop talking about her as if there is. She must be free to be herself.'

He was silent. He stretched his arms above his head, took a deep breath and walked around the room a little. Then, in a much calmer, softer, gentler way, he spoke again:

'Gracie, love – it's really important that you're *both* allowed to be yourselves.'

I supposed I should have been grateful, seeing as according to Uncle Freddy there were apparently millions of other grown-ups out there forcing their children to be people that they were not.

Bee was experimenting with her imagination, as creative people were inclined to do, he explained later. From the window I watched Bee in her fairy dress playing in the garden, fake wings flapping as she leapt around.

'It'd be much better if you stopped worrying,' said Uncle Freddy. 'Her behaviour's fine – if anything it's a sign of great intelligence. She'll grow out of some of it.' We both gazed out at her. She was lying in the grass now, holding a very patient Louie in the air with her feet and arms.

I knew there was no point in quarrelling, but at the same time, I didn't think Bee would ever grow out of the strange things she did, not without some serious intervention. I knew that if my parents were still alive they'd be doing something about her. They'd be worried about her like I was.

Most people aren't that thrilled about Mondays, but I more or less cherished them. OK, I might have had to go on a massive search for Bee's scarf and her gloves and all the things she'd lost, and needless to say I'd have to walk with her and listen to her babbling about the ridiculous things she believed, but when we got to school, she would skip off through the gates into her side and I'd head over to mine and I'd feel nothing but relief.

All the other people in my school were clear-water kids. They never had dark thoughts, or if they did they were able to swat them away and keep flapping about in the shallows all fresh and happy and trouble free.

Chris Crosby lived on the corner of Sorrento Road and Coliemore in a sandstone house with a black, shiny front door. I wasn't the only one who loved him. Practically everyone did. A vanilla ice cream kind of love: smooth, cool, simple, delicious, with tiny specks of something else – something dark and unattainable.

Up until recently, he'd had a perfect girlfriend whose name was Eva Doone. When Chris and Eva split up, the news went round the whole school like a Mexican wave.

Everyone was watchful and vigilant. Eva had not been ejected from his gang. She kept on going to the top table with the top group, but she wasn't sitting right beside him any more.

'What's the top group?' Bee had asked me and Scully, listening in on our conversation as usual the day after the news had broken. She stood wide-eyed and appalled-looking as we tried to explain.

'Why are you staring at us like that?' I asked, annoyed.

'Sorry,' she said. 'It's just . . . well . . . I'm striving to understand the concept.'

'What's to understand?' Scully asked. 'Top group. In control. Have their own table at lunch that nobody else is allowed to eat at. Don't talk to anyone else except each other. Better, thinner, richer, funnier, cleverer and more good-looking than everyone else. They have their own exclusive rituals. Cosmet Shopping Centre on Saturdays. And the top boys always get the best lockers and stuff, and the top girls wear make-up at school, even though it's not allowed. Nobody says a word to them. They more or less get to do what they like.'

'How horrifying,' said Bee. 'And how come everyone puts up with that?'

'Welcome to the world, Bee,' said Scully bitterly.

'Well, in my world all people are equal, and top groups that exclude other people are not allowed.'

Scully and I looked at each other. There was no point in continuing the discussion.

Uncle Freddy and Granddad said the door of our house was always open – to all our friends – as though there were great crowds of people waiting somewhere, dying to hang out with us. New friendships were more complicated than most people thought. Especially in my case, with no parents and unconventional guardians and a weird little sister. Scully was different – he was used to us.

'Your friend of four winters!' Bee said one day, as if I needed to be reminded how long I'd known him. We'd met in the library on a dark Saturday morning after Uncle Freddy had forgotten to pay the electricity.

'It's so very wonderful to see young people like yourselves availing of the resources here!' one of the Allen sisters who ran the library would always say when Bee and I arrived, and, 'Tell all your friends!' when we were leaving.

But I didn't have any friends, apart from Scully. And most other people I might have wanted to hang out with weren't that likely to show up at the library, especially now that Cosmet was the new place. It was well known by then that the top group had started to hang out there on Saturdays. People had seen Eva Doone and Ingrid Cleaver wafting through the top floor of the mall or sipping their skinny lattes in the company of the top boys. I wasn't interested in being one of the spectators. Plus you needed spare money to go there, so obviously I never did.

Anyway, Chris Crosby and his friends were out of my league. I didn't have the slimmest chance of getting to know them. I was OK about it. I never dreamed it would be any different. But random things sometimes happen and, when they do, they can make impossible things happen too.

THREE

It had taken 'much grit', as Granddad called it, and years of saving, but she had made her dream come true: Janine's nail and beauty bar was finally opening in the village.

'I couldn't be prouder of you, Janny, not if you were my own daughter,' Granddad said the morning of the launch.

Uncle Freddy was helping with the joinery and putting the finishing touches on the sign above the shop. Everybody was invited. We were at the top of the list. In honour of the event, Janine was planning a 'live demo' of the brilliant things that make-up can do. She asked me if I'd like to be her model for the afternoon.

'Oh, I'm not sure about that,' said Uncle Freddy, 'Grace doesn't wear make-up. You're not into that sort of thing, are you, Gracie?'

'Fred, don't be such an old bore,' Janine scolded. 'Let her decide about it for herself. Aren't you always going on about how they have to make their own decisions, do their own thing? Besides, she has the perfect face.'

I hated my face. I didn't think it was perfect for anything.

But I thought about Eva Doone and Ingrid Cleaver and how they always broke the rules and wore make-up and how nobody ever said a word to them about it, and they always looked great, and I thought about how I'd never even owned so much as a tube of lipstick.

'Yeah, Uncle Freddy, let me decide.'

It was easy. All I had to do was sit still in this high swivel chair with my back to the mirror and a plastic cape draped over my shoulders. The guests ate little sausages and miniature quiches and clinked their glasses together while they watched. Scully and Bee stood at the front frowning as Janine worked, crouching with her face very close to mine and then standing back, and then coming close again, ignoring everything else, spending ages getting it right.

When she was finished, she pulled off the cape with a gleeful flourish.

The whole crowd inhaled.

'Wow,' sighed Scully, but he didn't look that happy. He looked kind of troubled.

Janine twirled me round to face the mirror then. I just stared and stared. Everyone in the room clapped and raised tall sparkling glasses in the air.

32

It felt as if I was looking at someone who was not me. Someone beautiful.

Bee was definitely not one bit happy either.

'Please take it off,' she begged. 'I don't like it.'

But a sort of thrill was growing inside me, and it was such a great, uplifting kind of feeling that I didn't want it to go to waste. For the rest of the launch I kept catching my face in the mirrors all over Janine's new shop, and each time I was startled again by how I looked.

As instant as the striking of a match, a strange sort of mood had descended on me. I felt exotic and soft. I felt a heaviness too – as if someone had suddenly wrapped a cloak around me that was made of something rich, like velvet. It wasn't arrogance. And I didn't think it was vanity. Maybe you could call it relief. It was a feeling of freedom that people sometimes get when they put on a disguise.

There was darkness in my eyes and smoothness on my skin and a kind of golden shimmer on my cheeks, and as the minutes went by, those apparently shallow things turned me into someone new, someone who wanted to do new things that I'd never done before.

And I supposed I could never fully explain it, but that was probably why I grabbed my bike and headed out, telling everyone I'd be back in a while.

'Somebody please stop her!' wailed Bee. 'Her face has changed. It's most disturbing. I want her back the way she

33

was.' I could hear Bee's shouting, but I didn't care, and nobody did stop me.

I'd told Scully that I needed some fresh air. But in my head I'd already decided where I was going. I cycled all the way to Cosmet, locked my bike in the car park and made for the lights and the buzz.

Maybe I'd already had some unformed and silent idea about what I wanted, and who I was looking for. But there wasn't anything deliberate about what grabbed me that day. Bumping into Chris Crosby was an accident. At least that was what it felt like.

Cosmet was a bright and glaring and loud and twinkly place. I jumped on the giant escalator floating slowly as it took me upwards, and again I looked at myself in the glass, amazed each time at the person that Janine had turned me into.

At first I thought I was imagining it, but as I got closer, it was clear that Chris Crosby was standing at the top, looking straight at me, right into my eyes. We'd never spoken. He'd never even looked anywhere in my vague direction.

'Hey, hey,' he said, and at first I didn't answer so he said it again and came closer still.

'Me?' I replied, as casually as I could manage.

'Yeah, you. Listen, I hope you don't mind me asking you this, but could you do me a favour?'

'Eh, OK, sure,' I said.

34

'See, the thing is, my ex is just about to come out of Hollister. Would you mind walking by there with me?'

'Eh, no problem,' I answered, trying to look all relaxed and unflustered even though my whole body was heating up.

'Great. Excellent. And one more thing.'

'What?'

'Would you mind holding my hand?'

Would I mind? Holding Chris Crosby's hand?

'Well, I suppose that would be OK,' I said.

'Brill, thanks. Right then, no time to lose – let's go.'

And that was when Chris Crosby grabbed my hand in his – warm and wide and strong – and we dashed up to the next floor. We walked together as he whispered at me, 'Her name's Eva Doone. She goes to my school.'

I was too amazed to tell him I already knew what her name was and where she went to school. And where she sat at lunch. And what she looked like. And what she wore. And what she ate. And what she drank.

'It's all cool. Totally amicable. Like, we'd been together too long. But still, I wouldn't want her thinking I'm nursing some kind of broken heart or anything.'

I nodded and scrabbled around my brain, trying to think of something to say next but I was too shocked to talk and he was going to think I was a weirdo.

'Hey, sorry,' he said then. 'Should have introduced myself. I'm Chris. Chris Crosby.'

'I know.'

'You know?'

'I go to your school too. I'm in your class.'

'Get away!' he said, still holding my hand but stretching our arms out as far as they would go so he could look me up and down again. 'Really? I find that hard to believe. I mean, I'm pretty sure I'd have noticed you. What's your name?'

'Grace. Grace McAuliffe.'

He looked at me blankly, blinked a slow blink and said, 'Yeah, oh yeah, I recognise you now,' but I wasn't sure that he did.

The ambush came suddenly.

Somebody jumped on Chris Crosby's back, and somebody else came sliding into him on their knees, whacking against his shins, knocking him over. I screamed. There was a tangle of long legs and arms right there on the floor of the shopping centre. If I'd have been thinking straight, I'd have probably called the police.

'Calm down!' he laughed.

'Grace, meet Jack and Norm, my so-called friends.' Jack Eff and Norm Scallion jumped and whooped and laughed around us and I did my best to laugh too as I wrapped my head around the misunderstanding.

Jack and Norm didn't know who I was either. 'Crazy!' they said when I told them. There was no sign of Eva Doone. 'She left ages ago, man. Did you not get my text?' said Jack to Chris, who changed the subject.

We went for coffee. The three of them spent the whole time talking about a school ski trip that I hadn't even heard about.

'Really good value. Only a thousand a head.'

'Wow,' I said.

'We're all in,' said Chris. 'You?'

'Maybe,' I lied. He stared at me for so long then that I had to look away. After that, Norm and Jack started flicking rolled-up bits of straw wrappers at each other until someone came over to ask them to stop.

'I'm sorry about these lunatics. They don't get out much,' Chris said and I told him it was OK, neither did I.

'Well, you're much more civilised than them.'

'Hey, do you want to come back to my house to hang out with us some more?'

But by then I felt shy and speechless and unsettled again.

'No, no thanks. I have to go home,' I said, which by then was kind of true.

'Right, well, thanks for being such a good sport – you know, being my decoy and stuff,' he said. 'And I guess I'll see you on Monday.'

'Where?' I said, stupider than someone who actually had no brain.

'At school, silly.'

'Oh yes, yes. Right. See you, then.'

*

I must have cycled home but I couldn't remember it. All I did remember was realising that Janine was going to have to teach me to put on make-up, because from that moment I couldn't go to school without it on ever again.

Janine gave me tons of free samples. I sat in front of my mirror on Monday morning and made my face look almost as good as Janine had.

'Em, what the actual hell?' was what Scully said when I met him outside school.

'What do you mean?'

'I mean, what's with the new and totally unrecognisable face?'

'Excuse me, I have a right to do what I want. It's not your face, it's mine.'

'OK, OK, calm down,' he said. 'It's just a bit surprising – that's all.'

'Scully, this *is* me now. I mean, it's the new me. I'm fairly sick of the old version and I like this one a good bit better. It's the way I want to be from now on. I like it. So mind your own business.'

In English Chris Crosby leaned over from the desk behind me and slipped a folded piece of paper into my pocket, and pressed his fingers against my hip.

'I don't have your number. Send immediately,' said the note, with his mobile number and just his initials at the bottom. And in the corner of my eye there was a shadow, as if someone else was there too, standing just out of sight, but when I turned to look, the shadow was gone.

I didn't have a phone and so I thought my chances with Chris were pretty much doomed. But it turns out, they were not. It's kind of a long story, but between one thing and another, within a few weeks, I ended up becoming Chris Crosby's actual girlfriend.

Different people reacted differently to the news.

'Oh my God, you guys are sooooo cute,' Eva Doone screamed when she found out, appearing to have completely recovered from their breakup. And Ingrid agreed.

When Scully called after school one day, we sat drinking tea at the kitchen table. I couldn't wait to tell him. But when I did he said, 'Right, and what do you want me to say, exactly?'

'I want you to be happy for me.'

'Why would I be happy about that?'

'Because, Scully, this is the first time that anything has gone right for me in basically my whole life, and you're my friend, and there's no one else I can tell and . . . well . . . I really like him.'

'Why are you whispering?'

'I don't want Bee to hear. I think he could actually be my soul mate.'

'Chris Crosby? Your soul mate?' Scully asked and then

he coughed a grim and sceptical kind of cough. 'The guy doesn't even *have* a bloody soul.'

'Of course he does. Don't be like that. He likes me and he has a heart and a soul like everyone else. I'm still in shock.'

'That makes two of us,' mumbled Scully, and before I had a chance to ask him what he meant, Bee and Louie drifted into the kitchen, so we had to talk about something else.

My relationship with Chris put me into a state of almost constant astonishment, which was not a particularly helpful state to be in when you were doing your best to deserve your place in the top group.

It was hard to be all laid-back and cool while underneath I felt so jittery and scared of getting something wrong. Chris wasn't ever scared of anything. He kept on doing what he always did: being the centre of attention; holding court at the top table; captaining the rugby team; smiling; winning; shining.

It felt as if the whole school leaned in his direction when he passed by. When he walked through the door, every girl in our class gazed, propping their chins up with their hands.

'I am his actual girlfriend,' I kept saying to myself. One evening at home I must have accidentally said it out loud.

'Whose actual girlfriend are you?' Bee had asked.

Telling her was potentially disastrous, but she was the most persistent person I'd ever known. She wore me down in an infuriatingly monotonous voice. So in the end I told her.

'Chris. Chris Crosby.'

'Who is he again?'

'Eh, Bee, he's the leader of the top group, remember? Only the most gorgeous, popular, spectacular guy in the whole school. We're together. It's official.'

'And what precisely does that mean?'

'I mean, he asked if I'd be his girlfriend and I said yes. And because he's so brilliant and fabulous, I'm starting to feel quite brilliant and fabulous too.'

Bee frowned and disappeared for a while, claiming she had 'a small bit of thinking' to do.

'Gracie,' she said when she returned, 'do you really think that's how it works?'

'How what works?'

'You know, a boy randomly inviting someone to be his girlfriend and then someone saying yes and then that someone feeling fabulous?'

'Yes, this is generally the way things happen,' I explained.

'Sounds pretty stupid if you ask me,' she said.

'Yeah well, nobody *is* asking you. And anyway, what do you know?'

'I know a very great deal.'

'Like what?'

41

'Like that people shouldn't have to wait around for boys to ask them to be their girlfriends. And people should feel good about themselves no matter whether some big, fantastic, popular guy is interested in them or not.'

'Oh really, and how do you know that?'

'Grandfather Patrick told me, and Louie agrees, and so does Pale Emily.'

'Listen, Bee, for one thing, you can't possibly know whether Louie agrees or not, because he's a dog. For another thing, you have no right to go telling my secrets to Granddad without my permission. And who on earth is Pale Emily?'

'She's this girl. I met her on the beach. *She* sleeps in Dillon's Park, under the ground, and nobody tells *her* not to. In a cave. She smells of the earth.'

'Oh God, Bee, really? Nobody sleeps in a cave in the park. There's no such person as Pale Emily. Nobody has a name like that. Could you do me a favour and try from now on not to make things up?'

'I'm not making her up. She's real. We're friends.'

I was glad Chris Crosby and the others didn't know I had a sister because they would definitely all think she was a weirdo. It was easy enough for them not to know. Between her primary school and our secondary there was a safe distance – football pitches and a basketball court and quite a long laneway. There wasn't much of a chance of me bumping into her.

The best way to get Uncle Freddy to do stuff was to tell him we were disadvantaged. The important thing was actually to use that word – that or 'deprived' – and it helped if you said the words slowly, stretching them out, keeping your voice low and despondent. I felt bad about it, but on the plus side it worked wonders when it came to getting things we wanted. It was why Uncle Freddy had bought Bee her own dictionary, so ginormous that it doubled up as a step for climbing into bed. She'd seen it in the bookshop and said it would be a dream come true to own a book 'with all the words in it'. She'd begged for weeks, and cried tears of joy when one day, for no particular reason, he'd brought it home.

Bee's two favourite places were the bookshop and the library. She was for ever begging me to take her to one or the other.

'Oh goodness gracious me, but I do love the library! The Misses Allen are the best people ever,' Bee said. 'And reading a library book is basically the most magical thing you can do.'

'What do you mean?'

'It connects you!' she exclaimed, 'by an invisible thread! To all the other people who have already held that book in their hands in the past, and all the other people who will hold it in their hands in the future! How wonderful is that?'

'It's not wonderful. It's not even true, Bee,' I said.

There was no point in arguing. Bee believed what Bee believed, no matter what I did to try to set her straight.

We used our claims of being disadvantaged to persuade Uncle Freddy to let us eat dinner in our bedroom, even though he said it was totally against his principles. Bee would hug him and tell him how great he was, and she'd say that even though we were deprived, at least we had him, and his brown face would crinkle into a smile and all his principles would go flying out the window.

Uncle Freddy went along with the things Bee said and the stories she made up, and so did Granddad. In fact they both pretended to believe every word that came out of her earnest, innocent, animated mouth. They pretty much expected me to put up with Bee's delusions too. 'Don't be so hard on her, Gracie,' Uncle Freddy would say. 'It's not as if she's doing anyone any harm.'

FOUR

The storm came quickly and by surprise. Bee and I were both lying on our stomachs reading one night when we heard a rumbling from way off in the distance, and soon thunder, so big and loud that it shook the house and pummelled our bodies.

Saucepans clattered and glasses clinked in the cupboards and Louie began to howl, rushing up and down the stairs and in and out of our room, over and over again.

'No more fretting out of you lot,' said Uncle Freddy. 'Get into bed.' He ruffled Bee's hair as she clasped her little white-knuckled hands together and looked towards the window biting her lip.

When we got into bed, the weather had grown even more violent. It didn't seem as if it would ever stop. Lightning bleached Bee's shocked, wakeful face as she sat up, straight-backed and still.

'What is it, Bee?' I asked, hearing her breath going in and out faster than anyone's ever should.

'It's angry ghosts who we cannot see, Gracie,' she whispered anxiously.

'What?'

'Lots of them. All over the place. They haunt the coastline. Once in a while they get these terrible fits of fury. Tonight's the worst I've ever heard them. Scary lady is one of them, I think.'

Bee's face lit up and disappeared and lit up again as the lightning kept flashing and the storm blew outside. Thunder boomed around us as if there were big things falling from the sky.

'Beebee, honestly now. Lie down please, and no more of this. I can't be associated with all the weirdness, OK? Not any more. It really does have to stop.'

'Whatever can you possibly mean?'

'I mean you believing in ghosts along the coastline and scary ladies with no hair, and girls called Pale Emily and thinking that Louie talks to you. Can't you tell how ridiculous it all is?'

She propped herself up on her elbows and stared over at me looking betrayed. But I'd started explaining something to her and she needed to hear it, so I felt I might as well keep going.

'It really would be enormously handy if you didn't go round telling your mad stories any more. Do you think you

46

could try to do that for me? You don't realise how strange they sound, and how . . . well . . . stupid.'

'Mad? Strange? Stupid? I haven't the foggiest notion what in heaven's name you're talking about,' she replied and suddenly she was out of bed, hopping towards the door on one leg.

'Where are you going?'

'I'm rescuing Louie.'

'From what?'

'The terror.'

'Why are you hopping?'

'Because I feel like it.'

The windows rattled and shook and I sighed a weary sigh.

A few seconds later she came back with a shivering Louie.

'Shush, Louie, you mustn't be frightened, it's not allowed,' she soothed, darting an unfriendly glance at me. 'Anyway, it's only the peevish ghosts having their tantrums. They'll calm down in a while. They always do.'

It isn't easy to sleep when there is a storm raging outside your house and when you share your room with a ghost-believing sister and a heavily snoring dog.

Next morning the whole town was a total mess of damage, but the wind was gone and the sea was flat again. The battered trees were still. School was closed.

'It's the happiest day of my life,' said Bee.

We stayed at home and the people came out to sweep up the debris and cut off the dangerous broken branches, all dangling and splintered. They fixed the smashed windows and reattached the swaying gutters.

'Oh dear, those ghosts. Honestly. So wanton. So destructive. So full of that terrible rage,' sighed Bee. 'I do hate it so. And every time I see a broken window I get a terrible feeling of dread and sadness, I don't quite know why.'

I did my best to ignore her.

Back in school on Tuesday, Chris Crosby leaned across the desk. 'Hey, gorgeous, I've missed you,' he whispered and something warm and fire-like flickered inside me.

Being Chris Crosby's girlfriend came with lots of privileges. I got to sit at the top table. People began to smile at me and say hello by the lockers and they looked right into my face and not in a bad, brooding or indifferent way but with openness and hope. Nobody jostled or pushed me any more. Suddenly everybody knew my name.

It was actually kind of great.

Soon, it felt as if I'd never had lunch anywhere else – which was the amazing thing about how quickly new habits can become part of you.

'Hey, stranger. How's life at the top treating you?'

It was Scully.

'It's great. How are you? Come join me for lunch?'

Scully's face got a little brighter. 'Where?' he said.

'You know, the table where I sit with Chris and his friends?'

'Oh yeah, what a realistic proposal,' he said, his face darkening again. I pretended I didn't know what he meant, but of course I did. There had always been something forbidding about the top table. I could still hardly believe that I, Grace McAuliffe, got to sit there now.

'I miss you, Scully. I haven't seen you for ages.'

'Yeah well, I'm still here. I haven't gone anywhere.' The bell rang and he began walking off to his next class, still looking over his shoulder. 'You're the one who's disappeared.'

Next day, I was just sitting down with the others for lunch when I saw her coming. Beginning as a little dot way off in the distance, Bee's crazy shape was approaching, dashing towards the top table, her arms and legs flinging out in random directions the way they often did whenever she ran. A special kind of horror churned inside me as I waited for her increasingly inevitable arrival.

'Oh, Gracie,' Bee panted when she finally reached us, 'I'm so delighted I've caught you!' The others looked on with vague, slightly bored smiles.

'Who is this?' asked Chris.

I said, 'Oh no one, never mind,' and jumped off the table and grabbed Bee by the wrist before she had a chance to say anything else. I marched her away to where nobody would hear.

'What are you doing?' I whispered. 'You're not supposed to leave your yard.'

'Quite right,' she said, 'and as you know, under normal circumstances I wouldn't dream of it, but, Gracie, this is an emergency of gargantuan proportions!'

'What is?'

'It's the Misses Allen! They came to our class today looking for volunteers but nobody's available. They need our help. The storm ghosts have done so much damage. Opening hours are under threat! Can you believe such a disaster?'

It was then that I knew for sure it was the Misses Allen who had put the idea of ghosts into Bee's head. Local ghosts. Who affected the weather. Honestly.

'Bee, listen to me, please. The Misses Allen are mad. They're constantly making up all sorts of total nonsense. I think it's their way of looking for attention. What happened on Sunday night was a natural disaster. There are no ghosts. There isn't anyone after them. Nobody can create a storm. There's no force behind it. It's only nature.'

'Oh ho ho, of course that's what they want you to think.'

Bee's little voice had risen to such a volume that I could

see Jack and Chris way off in the distance turning their heads in our direction.

'OK, OK, Bee, give it a break, will you? You need to get back to class. The bell's about to ring.'

'I'm not leaving,' she said, holding me by the shoulders and looking deep into my eyes, 'not until you promise you'll come and help us. Not moving – watch me here, not moving a muscle.'

Chris had begun walking towards us. Panic is always a great way of getting me to commit to something.

'OK then, yes.'

'Yes, what?'

'Yes, I'll come.'

'Saturday, first thing?'

'First thing.'

'Promise.'

'I promise.'

'Woo hoo!' shouted Bee.

'I'll only come if you go back to school without delay, as in *right now*.'

She started running backwards towards the junior school, flinging her arms and legs, and shouting back at me as the distance stretched between us.

'The Misses Allen will be so pleased! I can't wait to tell them. I knew we could count on you.'

'Stop running like that!' I called to her. 'You'll fall!'

She blew me an extravagant kiss, turned to face the

right direction and skipped off towards the lane. I watched her the whole way as her mad figure darted across the basketball courts and into her side of the school.

'Who was that?' asked Chris.

'Oh her,' I said, all nonchalant and elusive. 'Just this kid I know.'

'You two, no more chat please. Everyone else is in their classrooms. Come on!' It was Mr Sanders. He was normally outlandishly annoying, but that day I was grateful to him for saving me from having to reveal the truth to Chris – which was that Bee McAuliffe was my sister, my closest relative, my flesh and blood, and she was never going to leave me alone.

FIVE

Apart from the photos, and the card that Bee had found, we didn't have anything belonging to my parents – I mean nothing solid, nothing I could hold in my hands. There were a few pale feelings like the brilliant scratchiness of Dad's hug and my mum's hand on my cheek and the echoes of her singing. I remember how she smelled too. Roasted almonds. Melted marshmallows.

Sometimes I still smelled that smell – and when I did, I'd scrunch up my eyes and imagine that she was right there in the room with me. I knew it was stupid, because of course she never was. And once in a while, I'd keep seeing these shimmery kinds of shapes in the corner of my eye. But whenever I turned to look at them, the shapes had always gone. I came to believe that they were the fuzzy, faded memories of my parents.

Memories don't feel like real things. They are more like ghosts, which are no use to anyone as far as I'm concerned:

the way they appear unexpectedly; the way they wobble at the edges of your sight; the way they are invisible to everyone else but at the same time, annoyingly inclined to pop up at a moment's notice out of nowhere and to leak into everything you do.

It was kind of embarrassing the way Bee loved everyone so extravagantly, but I think she loved our granddad most of all. She thought he was the best person of all time.

Sometimes I'd watch them from the house – how easy and complete the two of them looked with Louie always swirling around in a way he never did when I was with him. It was as if he sensed that they contained exciting, interesting, special things – things that I did not have.

'What do you two talk about all day down there by the sea?' I asked Bee once.

'All manner of things,' she replied cryptically. 'Grandfather Patrick knows everything. He has special powers. I believe him to be immortal.'

'Bee, please, you mustn't say things like that, and you mustn't believe them.'

But she gave me her knowledgeable look, with her lips pressed together and her arms crossed, which was always a signal to me, and a reminder: once Bee had made up her mind it was very hard for anyone to change it.

*

Every Christmas, Uncle Freddy and Granddad Patrick had a massive party. Uncle Freddy would invite Janine and Granddad Patrick would invite Lal and Gertie and all of his poker friends and Bee and I would invite Scully. Uncle Freddy would make the same speech, referring to our parents in a kind of code, saying, 'Yes, we've had our sadnesses. Indeed we have. But here is proof, if ever we needed it, that wonderful things can grow out of even the darkest of times. In some ways dark times can be the best thing that ever happened.'

And then the eyes of everyone at the party would glance at us, half horrified and half delighted at the love-filled tactlessness of Uncle Freddy's thinly veiled words.

'Don't get me wrong,' he'd always say. 'I mean, of course there have been terrible times and great losses. But you see without them, then these two . . .' and here he'd point at us with his thumbs . . . 'wouldn't be with me, and nothing better could have possibly happened to me than them.'

He claimed his life had been out of control until he'd come back to mind us. He said if it hadn't been for us, goodness knows where he'd be now. Bee always looked proud and smug whenever he said that.

'People think I saved them, but you know, the truth is quite the opposite, it is they who saved me.'

'We are his salvation,' Bee whispered very loudly to me in front of everyone.

Personally I didn't want to be the reason for anyone's salvation, not even Uncle Freddy's.

All I wanted to be was a normal, ordinary person.

He would say other things too, like how neither of us had ever given him a moment's trouble, only gladness and enchantment.

Joy was what we were, and a gift, and an absolute treat to have around. And yes, OK, it was nice to be told what brilliant people we were and to be seen as such special gifts and all that. But the real truth was I would have preferred something else.

'Do you miss them?' Scully had asked one Christmas when we'd escaped from the grown-ups and were out in the garden with our backs on the grass, looking at the sky.

'No. I mean, not really,' I'd said, not quite sure how to talk about them at all.

But the truth was, I often found myself wishing for my parents back – not always because of grief or anguish, even if little hints of such things did appear every so often inside my brain. No, I wished them back because they had been normal, and Uncle Freddy and Granddad Patrick and Bee, well, they definitely were not.

Even our parents' names had been average and ordinary. I often said them under my breath just to hear what they sounded like.

'Daniel.'

'Barbara.'

56

And I began to remember that when they were alive, the house was always tidy, the beds made tight and smooth, and in my head after all, there was the faint flickering picture of my mum lighting candles when we had dinner and lovely music always playing in the background.

Scully said he was kind of jealous of us.

'What do you mean, Scull?'

'Well, Fred and Patrick just think the two of you are complete jewels. It never feels ordinary to be here. It always feels kind of special.'

A lot of people think that everyone spends their lives wanting to be special, extraordinary, outstanding. But to be honest, if you really think about it, it's the opposite. At least it was for me.

'I don't want special. I want normal,' I said back, more loudly than I'd meant to.

'Come on, Gracie, we don't have time for your stupid make-up,' Bee had whined on the Saturday we were getting ready to help at the library. But she was just going to have to wait, because I was going out in public and it was a small village and there was a very strong chance that I might bump into Chris or some of the others.

'You look absurd,' Bee said.

'That's your opinion,' I replied.

'Yes, it is,' she said, 'especially considering we're going

to be involved in quite hard labour today, and you look as if you're going to the opera.'

I didn't care. And I didn't expect her to understand.

For some time, the Misses Allen had been mentioning 'disappearances' and 'occurrences' and inexplicable windy draughts creeping in from nowhere that knocked things over including the great vase at the entrance that they liked to fill with fresh flowers. On a still and windless day it had shaken and wobbled and fallen over, smashing into a thousand splinters. It had been worth an absolute fortune and it was very lucky, the Misses Allen said, that they'd had the good sense to have it insured.

With the money they got, they'd refurbished their shelving and replenished some of their dwindling stocks and had had a huge gathering with cake and tea and little muffins with icing in the shape of books on top of them. That had been months ago, when no one could have predicted the damage that the weather was going to do.

The night of the storm, one of the new shelves, sturdy and well built, came crashing to the ground. All the A and B authors got strewn around everywhere in the dark.

The big double front doors had both been broken and were leaning off their hinges like drunk people half-heartedly trying to get into a party. When we arrived, one of the Misses Allen was ordering two friendly workmen around in a very loud voice. The other was mixing a huge tin of paint. A row of clean new brushes was lined up on a tray, waiting for us. 'Oh jolly good!' they said. 'We'll have this job done in no time at all.'

My heart sank. Helping *inside* the library was what I'd signed up for. I didn't know we'd be outside at the front for all to see, painting the new door. As the door was hung and the paint got mixed, the two of them bustled around in their purple and orange shawls and their pale blue stockings and their sensible old-lady shoes.

Any other time of the week would have been better, but in the middle of a Saturday morning there was no knowing who might pass by.

I was pretty much stuck there for the day. I'd promised to support them. Bee and the Misses Allen never doubted anyone for a second, and when someone doesn't doubt you, it makes it all the more important that you do the things you promise.

Sure enough though, we'd hardly got started when Chris whizzed by on his skateboard. I prayed that he wouldn't notice us, but of course he did.

'Hey, Gracie!' He smiled.

I looked like an idiot.

'What you up to?'

'We're helping the Misses Allen,' I said, feeling kind of ashamed.

'Yes,' said Bee, 'smartening this poor old lovely place up after the cruel and pitiless storm.'

'Yes indeedy,' chirped the Misses Allen. 'These darling girls!'

I should have been cheered by their enthusiasm and passion, and proud of them for what they were doing, but Chris probably thought it was weird, and then I saw him recognising Bee who had come over and was standing beside me with paint spattered across her beaming face.

'Oh, you,' said Chris, and I realised he was talking to Bee. 'I've seen you before, haven't I?'

'Yes,' said Bee, all bright and chirpy, and then the two of them looked at me, waiting.

'Bee, this is Chris. Chris, this is Bee,' I mumbled, half hoping he wouldn't hear. Bee frowned at me.

'I'm her sister!' declared Bee.

Chris responded by saying, 'Wow, Gracie, really? You never said.'

'Didn't you?' added Bee, looking crosser still.

'Well, you know, I don't always have to tell people every detail of my life.'

He asked her how old she was and she told him.

'You must be in Katy's class,' he said.

More chat between the two of them. It turned out Chris had a little sister too, called Katy, something he'd never said either. Bee was delighted. She couldn't wait to go back to class so she could introduce herself.

'Great,' I thought. 'Exactly the last thing I need.'

Before he left, Chris pulled a strand of hair out of my eyes and said he'd see me soon. He winked at Bee. To my dismay, she winked back at him and he trundled off on his skateboard and again I wondered if my status as his girlfriend could ever possibly survive.

By then everybody was talking about the ski trip. For Chris and his gang it was an uncomplicated thing. They didn't need to ask each other if they were going. Boundless joy belonged to them. Endless fun was a basic right. The trip was theirs and so was the avalanche of Instagrams that it was going to generate.

I told Uncle Freddy about it over dinner. He looked at me gravely across the table munching on a mouthful of peas.

'Gosh, Gracie, this is a bit out of the blue and it seems very expensive. Are you sure it's something you'd like to do?' and I was about to tell him it was the only thing I wanted to do, but his fists were clenched around his knife and fork and the crease of his forehead was deep and crooked.

'Ah no,' I said, 'not really. I'd probably hate it.'

Uncle Freddy could barely stay on top of the bills as it was.

'What's that smell?' asked Janine who'd dropped in with a prescription for Granddad. She was right. There was a kind of putrid air around the house. After some investigating, Janine found what was causing it: bagsful of rubbish piled up, stretched and black and oozing in the back garden, along the side wall.

'Uncle Freddy's forgotten to pay the bin charges again.'

Was normality too much for someone to ask?

In my case, apparently so.

'You're not *going*?' said Eva, her voice as shocked as if I was planning to commit some kind of crime.

'No, I'm just not into it.'

'Not *into* it? Gracie, it's skiing. Ski. Ing. Everybody's into it.'

'It's a major pity you won't be there,' said Chris.

'What do you mean "pity"?' I replied.

'Well, you know, it's the kind of experience that you can't share with the people who don't go. You'd be a special part of the club if you came, and if you don't, well . . . then . . . you won't be. So, you know: pity.'

'It's not a pity as far as I'm concerned,' I said and my words came out angrier than I'd meant them to. 'I don't know why you keep saying that. There's nothing to feel pity about.'

'I didn't mean it like *that*,' said Chris, shifting around and staring past me. 'I'm not pitying you, if that's what you think.'

'It's not what I think, but maybe it's what *you* think, otherwise you wouldn't keep saying it.'

'Hey, Gracie?' he replied, his perfect forehead a sudden puzzled crinkle. 'Come on. Nobody is saying anything bad here. We just want you to come with us – isn't that right, everyone?' And Eva and Norm and Jack and Ingrid all nodded their heads but there was nothing about the way their faces looked that made me feel as if any of them really meant it.

'Yeah, no need to be so touchy,' added Eva. 'All we want is to share this great week with you, that's it. Nobody understands why you won't come.'

'Maybe you're too cool to hang out with us,' said Ingrid and that was when I knew they were mocking me for sure, because they were the coolest group in school. I was hanging out with them by a thread.

Chris smiled though and he walked back to class with me. 'I wish you'd trust us a bit more.'

'What do you mean?'

'Well, you need to start thinking of my friends as your friends. We just want you to be part of things. We want you to be OK.'

'I'm fine,' I said, 'it's everyone else who's the problem. I don't know why they can't just drop the subject.'

'OK, well, I'll tell them that then, Miss Grumpy Pants,' he said, and I tried my best to smile.

Nobody dropped the subject. They started taking selfies in their goggles at lunch every day.

'There's still time to change your mind.'

'You don't know what you're missing.'

'It's the best thing ever.'

'It's the reason we all became friends in the first place.'

It was hard to explain why I did what I did. It was just that I'd begun wishing and wishing things were different and that I *could* go, wishing that I didn't feel so much on the outskirts of everything. Wanting to be a proper, permanent part of the group, in my own right, not just because of Chris. The more they went on about it, the more something began to snap inside me.

'Come on, Gracie, come on, Gracie, change your mind, change your mind,' Chris started to say, and slowly the rest of them joined in until they were all saying it in a kind of chant.

And then there came the moment. I felt it happening and it was as if their chants had poured something into me: something full of dishonesty and longing.

'OK, OK, everyone,' I said, 'I'll go. If that's what it's going to take to get you all to shut up. I'll go.'

The top group rose to its feet with a great, collective noise of delight. Someone was standing still across the room. It was Scully. No one else seemed to notice him as everyone cheered and whooped. Chris pushed his broad strong fist into the sky the way he would if someone had done something heroic or important.

When I looked back again, Scully had gone.

The next day, Chris and Norm told me our deposits were due in by Friday. Two hundred and fifty quid.

SIX

The Misses Allen swam all year round. We sometimes went with them down to the beach. They'd pull out their giant swimsuits and their caps that were covered in huge shuddering rubber flowers and they'd wriggle into everything behind a stripy screen that they erected to protect their modesty. They would leap into the water without ever a moment's hesitation. 'That's the trick!' they'd shout to Bee and me, when only their heads were visible. 'No dilly-dallying – plunge right in. The water seems, of course, as if it's going to be very cold, but it's really not!'

Louie always surged in after them which made the Misses Allen shriek with delight and affection.

They had a theory that being strong swimmers was practically a compulsory part of life. They hadn't learned that, they said, until they were 'quite grown', and they exchanged this split-second secret look that the Misses Allen gave each other once in a while when they talked about certain things.

They looked exactly alike, so it wasn't surprising that everyone thought they were twins.

'Not so!' declared one of them when I made the same mistake.

'We are triplets, but sadly, there are only two of us still in the land of the living,' the other said without seeming sad at all, but stopping for a moment all the same, both of them seeming to forget what they were in the middle of.

I wondered what had happened to a third of them, but did not ask. When it came to the Misses Allen, there was mystery in some of the ways they spoke and in some of the things they said to each other. There was lots I didn't know about them, including that they were brilliant friends of Granddad.

'He has cracked the secret of living,' Bee announced the night before the big celebration that we and Uncle Freddy had arranged.

The next day was his birthday and he was going to be ninety.

Bee watched Granddad from our bedroom. I could see him humming away to himself. He was looking furtive and carrying something brown and bulky in his arms. He disappeared into the shed for a few minutes and for a second, I wondered what he was up to. When he came back out, he was holding a weapon. He began swinging his old arms wildly and with energy that I'd never thought I'd see in anyone, let alone someone of his age.

'What on earth is he doing out there with that machete? He'll cut one of his arms off.'

'It's not a machete, it's a scythe,' corrected Bee.

I'd been trying to encourage Bee to go to bed but she was busy explaining her theories about our grandfather and as usual had zero interest in sleep.

'I think it's highly possible that he is part of a team of magic people. His immortality is a great comfort to me, Gracie. In this world so full of endings, it's wonderful to know that Grandfather will always be here.'

'For the thousandth time, stop saying things like that.'

'Why, when it makes me so happy to say them?' she sang.

'Oh, Bee, because they're not true, and besides, I worry that you're getting your hopes up about things that can't possibly be facts. Nobody's immortal. Not even Granddad, however much you might like to believe it.'

I was always trying to give her advice and she always acted as if she was paying serious attention. But she never actually was.

Talking about death was an awkward thing in our house on account of the subject being completely taboo, but it didn't deter Granddad Patrick.

'Most of my friends are dead,' he proclaimed quite merrily in the middle of his birthday speech the next day.

'Thank goodness for the wonderful little Beebee here and Gracie and Fred and Janine. Thank goodness also for Jemimah and Celia!' He held up his glass in the direction of two people who'd just come through the door. It took me a while to recognise the Misses Allen who had huge coloured feathers in their hair, tied on with velvet hairbands, enormous netty dresses that rustled when they moved and make-up on their faces, which was something we had never seen on them before.

'I never knew they were friends with Granddad,' I whispered to Bee.

'Didn't you?' she said in this self-satisfied way that pretty much infuriated me, acting as if she knew everything, even though she was so much younger than me and as mad, basically, as a brush.

I began to suspect the Misses Allen were having some kind of old-person amorous thing with Grandfather, from the way they looked at him and how they laughed so loudly at even his not-very-funny jokes, and how much attention they paid to him by rubbing his arm and then kissing him, one cheek each, leaving huge smudges of lipstick on his face. Janine approached him with a tissue to rub it off.

'Goodness no, my dear!' said Granddad, gently evading Janine's best efforts.

'These are marks of romance and glamour!' he said,

peering delightedly into the mirror and then spending the rest of the evening declaring, 'I'll never wash my face again!' to the sound of the Misses Allens' uproarious laughter.

'Jemimah? Celia? Is that really what they're called?'

Needless to say, Bee said she'd always known but that it was not polite to call old ladies like the Misses Allen by their first names. 'As a matter of fact,' she said, 'I know loads more other things about them but I don't care to discuss any of it.'

'What do you know?'

She stood in front of me, all grown-up and straight-backed.

'Now is not the time, Gracie. We are celebrating Grandfather's wonderful, everlasting life! Plus we have to hand round nibbles for the guests.'

Granddad insisted on doing his party piece, which was singing a long and tuneless song with Louie, who howled along even more tunelessly beside him.

All through this agonising performance Bee's eyes glistened with pride and love. When he was finished and the applause had trickled out, she said in a huge loud whisper, 'Isn't he simply great? Thank goodness he's never going to die.'

Everyone heard, and everyone laughed.

So, when Granddad Patrick actually did die, Bee was

broken-hearted and sad and lost – along with the rest of us. But most of all she was astonished.

SEVEN

I t's not a phenomenon widely discussed, but death in your family feels like the world has kind of been jolted into a parallel universe. Without Granddad, food tasted funny. The house filled up with new, odd sounds and it smelled strange, and there were peculiar empty pockets of space all over the place – in the corners and at the top of the stairs – and unusual little gusts of breeze that seemed to curl in and out of his bookshelves and all those places that he used to linger. It's not only a person who dies. The spaces that he used to fill – it seemed as if they were dead and different too. Everybody felt it, especially Louie, who lay for a whole day pressed up against the part of the sofa where Granddad used to sit and then wandered around the house searching and searching, stopping only to sniff Granddad's silver-tipped walking stick.

'So much loss in their young lives,' said the Misses Allen at the funeral. Everyone kept on reminding us about how old he had been as if somehow it was supposed to stop us from being sad.

First the crowd settled into silence and then, unexpectedly, there was this flurry and rustle and people inside the church began to mumble and turn their heads towards the grand doorway.

'Oh no, here she is,' whispered Uncle Freddy.

'Who?' I asked.

'Your aunt. Lucy.'

'Aunt Lucy?' Bee had replied, too sad to be anything more than mildly quizzical.

'Yes,' said Uncle Freddy, but he didn't explain, and there was so much going on that I didn't bother telling Bee anything else.

'Something selfish this way comes,' Uncle Freddy said, a bitter edge to his voice, as the snaps of Aunt Lucy's high heels rang out into the air. Bee had insisted on bringing Louie of course, who started doing this low, quite frightening growl, and then Aunt Lucy was in front of us. She wore a hat with black netting. Seeing her face was like hearing an old forgotten song. She held her arms out as if she was expecting Uncle Freddy to hug her, which he did not do.

Louie's barks rose to a hysterical pitch and Bee was the only one who could soothe him.

In any case, it wasn't the time for proper introductions. Sad music was starting to play.

'What's with the ridiculous hat?' muttered Uncle Freddy but nobody answered him.

'I would very much like to do an official speech in honour of Grandfather,' said Bee self-importantly to Uncle Freddy, who said if that was what she wanted to do then she must. I was terrified.

Her head was barely visible above the podium, but her voice was steady and clear.

'Ahem,' she said, reading from a crumpled piece of paper. 'Grandfather Patrick's heart no longer beats. Air does not go in and out of his lungs as once it used to do, and his face is cold. We used to walk on the beach and he told me all his secrets. I will still walk, and I will remember all the secrets, but nothing is ever going to be the same. My grandfather and I had been working on an underground plan: he and I were going to camp in Dillon's Park. We were going to go night fishing under the stars. He made a secret promise to me because my parents are dead and nobody else will do it. But now he is dead too, and everything is changed for ever, and there is nothing to be done but put up with it. Thank you very much.'

Her words were followed by an awkward silence that was only broken by the priest suggesting that we offer each other the sign of peace. Bee went around to every single person in the church, shaking their hands and saying things such as, 'May you find solace in this time of great darkness,' and, 'I think it's possible that we're going to need more sandwiches.'

'I know I've only just met her, but I think there's something lovely about Aunt Lucy,' I said to Janine as everyone walked out of the church, not realising that Uncle Freddy was right behind us.

'Yeah well, that's what she wants you to think,' he replied.

I'd never want to besmirch his beloved memory, but when I really tried to figure out why Bee was the way she was, a lot of the blame had to fall with Grandfather Patrick. His old, eccentric ways had rubbed off on her. It was wrong of him to have made that promise. Whatever our chances had been of getting the Dillon's Park camping plan out of her head, those chances were now gone. She was never going to forget and she was never going to stop going on about it. They'd been a team, the two of them, from the moment she'd laid her head on his chest when she had been so small.

I thought about the gap he had left in our lives, especially Bee's. How she and he went almost daily to the beach together, with Louie on the lead, pulling them into a funny-looking trot. They always took a long time and they usually brought food because of the imaginary friend that Bee had invented called Pale Emily, who Bee claimed was often hungry. He believed all Bee's stories, and their walks were when she would tell him the crazy things inside her head that never seemed to shock or trouble him, and I couldn't stop thinking now about the sight of them both – him with his sturdy walking stick, her in an oversized raincoat with her bag full of goodies, and – on windy days – clinging delightedly to our old red kite.

Louie would whizz ahead, doubling back once in a while, and Bee and Grandfather Patrick would move at a slug's pace along the shore, stopping every few steps for Granddad to point to something high above their heads or for Bee to pick up a shell or stone on the sand at her feet so that they could examine it, or for both of them to stare out at the foam and glitter of the ocean.

The day before he died, Bee claimed she felt something, though she wasn't sure what.

'Everything feels different,' she had said, never imagining for a moment what was going to come. 'There is change afoot.'

I asked her what that could possibly mean.

'I don't know, but there is a fizz and a crackle in the air,' was all she said, as if that was any kind of an explanation. 'Can't you hear it? I must let it out.' And I remember how she had rushed from her bed to open the window.

*

After the funeral, everyone came back to the house. Uncle Freddy seemed to be raging with Aunt Lucy. He said this was typical of her, all late and bustle and surprise and

76

disruption and attention-seeking and deliberately stealing the thunder from the dead.

'She's been looking for attention all her life,' he said.

'Oh, Uncle Freddy! Really? Why would you say such mean things about someone who's come back to help us grieve for Granddad?'

'I can't help it,' he replied. 'It's called animus.'

'What is that?'

'A deep-seated dislike that is difficult to suppress and for which there is an undeclared but strangely logical basis,' said Bee, who had appeared from nowhere as usual, leaning into our conversation.

In spite of the animus, and regardless of the nasty reception from Louie, Aunt Lucy ended up becoming an unexpectedly central part of what Bee called Grandfather Patrick's Death Party. Every time she passed Louie, he did a low, sinister snarl. I ended up having to lock him in the utility room where he howled like a wolf, scratching frantically from inside.

'Oh gosh, I'm really very sorry,' I'd said. 'He's never this badly behaved.'

'Is that so?' said Aunt Lucy, who seemed more concerned about damage to the back of the utility room door than was reasonable for a visitor in someone else's house.

Uncle Freddy kept on not hugging her, but lots of

other people did. When Aunt Lucy approached Bee, Bee began to back away, looking appalled. I was mortified. To compensate, I made a massive deal out of telling Aunt Lucy that the spare room was all hers, to which Aunt Lucy replied, 'I know it is.'

'Don't you think that was a strange thing for her to say?' Bee whispered to me later in the voice of a secret accomplice. 'Whatever could she have meant by it?'

'People say odd things at funerals,' I replied. Though there wasn't much point in trying to explain that to Bee, who said odd things all the time.

Gallons of tea were served. Aunt Lucy pressed a hankie against her mouth whenever anyone introduced themselves or said how sorry they were about Grandfather Patrick and Bee wondered what she had to do with our granddad, but nobody explained it to her.

'Oh dear, oh goodness,' Aunt Lucy said after a while, flapping her hand close to her face. 'I'm sorry, but I'm suddenly feeling a bit dizzy.'

'Do you think you might like to go upstairs? I've made your bed and we could bring your luggage and you could unpack,' I suggested. 'Plus, it's quiet there.'

Aunt Lucy looked at me very deeply then.

'Grace, that is very kind of you. I'm really grateful to you for noticing.'

'This way,' I said, but I could see she already knew how to get to the spare room. I grabbed Bee on my way up.

'Someone has to stay with Aunt Lucy,' I told her.

'Why?'

'We can't leave her in a room on her own. She's very upset. She might need something.'

'Well, I've no intention of being left on my own with her, just in case that's what you think,' said Bee.

'OK, we'll both stay then,' I replied, feeling cross.

We followed Aunt Lucy to the top of our stairs, where Grandfather Patrick's walking stick leaned up against the bookshelf, knobbly and wooden and dark and shiny.

There was a stone in my chest. I thought of the millions of times Grandfather Patrick had pointed that stick out to sea or burrowed it into the sand to uncover a reprehensible piece of rubbish or a fabulous shell. His coat and hat were hanging on the hook in the upstairs hallway.

Bee reached out her hand and touched the sleeve and then buried her face in the folds and stood there with her face to the door.

'Please,' I begged silently to myself. 'Please, Bee. Be normal.'

But Aunt Lucy's attention was elsewhere. As soon as she had reached the top of the stairs, everything about her seemed to change. It was hard to describe, but her face, which had been rigid and taut, seemed to relax. Slowly she strolled over to the shelf on the outside of our bedroom door and, one by one, she picked up the little gargoyle heads that Uncle Freddy had made for us and she turned each of them around in her hand puckering her nose as if there was something about them that smelled bad.

'What are these?' she asked.

'Our gargoyles,' Bee said.

'Where did they come from?'

'It's none of your business—' replied Bee, so rudely that I had to interrupt.

'Uncle Freddy,' I said. 'He made them for us years ago.'

'Goodness. I can't imagine what possessed him to make such ugly, frightening-looking things.'

'Yes, well, we like them and we're not scared of them,' said Bee. 'Other people are – that's the whole point. They ward off ghosts and bad things and mean people. It's why he made them for us.'

She glared at Aunt Lucy.

Inside the spare bedroom, Aunt Lucy ran her hand along the top ledge of the mirror that hung in there, and then she looked at her fingers and clapped a few times, to get rid of the dust. There were heaps of coats on the chairs and piles of papers on the floor and I began to think we should have tidied up a bit more.

By then, Bee had turned around and was standing with her back to the door. Everything felt awkward and uncomfortable. I didn't know what to say. Aunt Lucy took a break from her inspection and looked at us for a few seconds, her eyes narrowing.

'Could somebody please get me another cup of tea?' she

said eventually. 'I really need that now. I do feel so very sad.'

'If you're so sad,' said Bee to my horror, 'how come this is the first time anyone has ever met you. Who are you?'

Aunt Lucy turned away from Bee. Her nostrils flared and there was steel in her face again.

'Oh no. This is exactly as I thought.'

'What? What did you think?' asked Bee, standing legs apart, hands on hips.

'You don't even know who I am,' said Aunt Lucy.

It should have been staring her in the face, but Bee was often blind to obvious things.

The doorbell went then and Bee and I raced each other down the stairs.

A load more people poured in through the hallway – old friends of Grandfather Patrick with bottles of wine, the Misses Allen who'd gone home to take bread and cakes out of their oven, and other people we did not know carrying big casseroles full of stew.

When Scully came, he stood at the gate looking into my face, and then he walked up the path and hugged me for a long time, not saying a word. He handed me a card.

Uncle Freddy put his arms around all the visitors and thanked them for their kindness and for coming. He was trying to look cheerful, but sad people have invisible weights pressing down on them and when they breathe in, it sucks air out of the room and everyone feels it.

Uncle Freddy told us we were to come back into the kitchen and forced us to discuss things we didn't care about to people we didn't know.

About twenty times, I was asked what year I was in at school and what subjects I was doing and what sports I liked to play. Nobody asked me how I was feeling about Granddad being dead, and they didn't ask Bee either.

Everyone mingled and helped with the food and I cleared up the empty plates and cups, and there was so much chat and noise in the house that it was a while before anyone realised that Bee had disappeared.

We called for her, and checked our bedroom, and looked in all the usual places.

'Everyone, stay calm! Nobody is to be worried,' said Uncle Freddy. 'Bee often goes missing. No need for any alarm.' And then he pulled on his jacket and went to the car much faster than someone who wasn't worried would have done.

I'd like to say I was thinking thoughts of love about her but all the time I was really thinking what a pain my sister was and wondering why I was the one who always ended up having to find her. I already knew where she was going to be.

I cycled to the library and threw my bike on the path in front of the door, leaving the back wheel spinning. And there they were – Bee and the Misses Allen – in the bright book-lined room, the three of them resting and reading on the soft beanbags. I had to use one of the Misses Allen's phones to ring Uncle Freddy and let him know Bee was fine. He sighed down the phone. The Misses Allen explained that they had found Bee in our garden, crying, and they'd decided to 'take her out of the equation' for a little while to help her 'collect herself'.

'I'll be right there,' said Uncle Freddy in a wobbly voice.

'No, don't worry, you go back to the party. I'll bring her home. I've got my bike. We'll be OK. It's probably done her good to be out of the house for a little while. I think the Misses Allen were right to bring her here, she just needed a break.'

'Bless you, Gracie,' he said and it felt good for a second to be the one who had found her and to be the one who was going to bring her home.

Bee was reading aloud to the Misses Allen from an old book whose name I could not see. Her eyes were red and her face was blotchy and I thought it was good that she'd been crying – she probably needed it.

There is only so much distracting people can do and only so much talk about irrelevant things before the black hole of loss and the burden of absence becomes impossible to carry, especially for someone like my sister. I felt glad that she had escaped for a while from the sandwiches and the cups of tea and the pats on the head.

'Nothing like a stroll around the treasure chests of

curiosity to help start to mend a grieving heart,' said the Misses Allen.

'Yes, thanks a million. But we should probably get back now. It would be odd of us to stay away for too much longer with all those people in the house.'

'Oh goodness yes, of course, how silly of us, we're terribly sorry,' they replied, not looking sorry in the slightest.

'Bee, my dear,' they said, patting her hands. You must go back.'

'Yes, I suppose I must,' said Bee, nodding her head.

The Misses Allen gathered around Bee and spoke to her in gentle, kind voices and they put some books in a bag and pressed it into my hands. 'Just a few stories of adventure and bravery and of overcoming impossible obstacles,' they explained and I thanked them because of all the people who needed stories like that right then, it was definitely us.

They saw us to the door and kissed us both on each of our cheeks and I thought for a moment I might ask if we could stay a little longer. 'You're going to survive. You're going to get through this, but you're quite right – you should go back now because your dear Uncle Freddy needs you both today more than ever.'

They stood waving, framed like a picture in the library's freshly painted doorway.

EIGHT

When someone is on the back of your bike, you can sense things about what's going on inside their heads that you mightn't have noticed before. As I sped back home, I could feel Bee's sad breathing. Twitches full of grief; fidgets soaked in sorrow.

'What? What is it?'

'Nothing,' she replied, too quickly.

'Hey, Bee,' I said, slowing down and then coming to a stop. 'Didn't you know that it's against the law to keep secrets from your sister?'

'Is it? Seriously?' she replied, sounding properly concerned.

'Yes, and it's about time you started telling me what's going on inside your head. Come on, isn't there anything you want to talk about?'

We were near our gate by then. In front of the house, the grass on the green had recently been cut and it smelled good. I thought it would be OK if we hung out there for a little while before going back in and having to be on good behaviour again.

'Come on, Bee, do. Talk to me.'

She missed him. It was as simple as that. They had been a strange team, Bee and Granddad, always chatting, always walking together on the beach, always chuckling away over some joke or another – 'thick as thieves', as Granddad would have said.

'You must be feeling very miserable,' I said, realising something for the first time about how deep her sadness was.

'Well . . . I was at first, but not so much now that I've had a talk with the Misses Allen.'

'Well, that's good, isn't it? What did they say to cheer you up?'

'They told me that I might be able to see Grandfather Patrick again.'

'Did they?'

'Yes,' she said, all matter of fact, and then she lay down on the grass and looked at the sky. 'Do you think that might be possible?'

I could hear hope shining in her voice, and I felt that what I said next was going to be important. I had a special responsibility to tell her the truth.

'Bee, I don't really know. I don't think anyone does.'

'Someone knows,' she replied. 'Or should I say, three people do: the Misses Allen and Louie.'

'OK, well, firstly, as I keep trying to tell you, Louie is not a person, he's a dog. And secondly, the Misses Allen might think they know, but honestly, truly, nobody does.'

'They DO. I know they do, and I don't understand why you're telling me that they don't. I find it terribly confusing,' she said. A ripple appeared on her chin. Her eyes shimmered again with tears.

'Look, I know this is hard, but you said it yourself at the funeral, Bee – there is nothing to be done. We are all going to have to get used to life without him. And the thing is, even if the Misses Allen are right, which they may well be, even if they are, even if you will see him again, it won't be for a very, very long time.'

'Well, again, that's where you're wrong, Gracie. I can see him very soon. The Misses Allen have told me.'

'What did they tell you?'

'I'm not supposed to say.'

'Hey, Beebee, you can say anything to me. When did they tell you you'll be able to see him?'

'Whenever I feel like it. Right now, this minute, if I want.'

'Oh yeah? Where?'

Bee held me by my shoulders in that stern way she did whenever she had something important to tell me, her face close to my face, her voice all serious and intense.

87

'OK, Gracie, if I tell you, will you promise to try to believe me and not make fun of me and not say this to anyone else?'

'I promise.'

Bee did an exaggerated clearing of her throat.

'There is this place, Gracie. The Misses Allen know all about it. Behind the wall in Dillon's Park, but nobody can see it any more because it's high up and all the gorse and bramble have grown around it.'

'Are you sure you're not thinking of a fairy tale? Sleeping Beauty's castle? Rapunzel's tower?'

'Oh, for goodness' sake, don't be so silly. I'm not a baby. I'm talking about something real here, Gracie. Real, strong and solid. Made of bricks and slate and glass and marble. You have to go up very, very far and high – along the topmost part of the cliff path that nobody is allowed on. The Misses Allen say it's terribly exciting when something has been hidden for years, because people stop believing it's true and then only a few people are in on the secret. Just because you can't see something doesn't mean it's not there, that's what they said. And I believe them.'

'What the actual heck?' I said, a clench of despair in my stomach.

'Gracie, I do wish you'd believe me. Most people are like you. They don't think it's real at all. They think it's only a legend or a story but it is not. People are afraid and suspicious of it and maybe they are right to be, but the thing is, you see, it is the place where you have a chance of seeing your dead people again, and in the case of Grandfather Patrick I'd very much like that.'

Bee's words grew thick then, with sadness I thought, and grief and loss, and I got angry because I did not want her to be stirred up by the sudden and deluded hope that the Misses Allen had filled her with. She stood and held her feet apart and plonked her hands on her hips.

'You see, I could not bear the idea that we wouldn't see him any more. I'm so relieved that the Misses Allen have told me about this place. It's called Hotel Magnificent. Magic, Gracie! Magic is real! I always knew, but the Misses Allen have confirmed it. We can go there. We can meet up with him. Oh, it's so great. I can't tell you how fantastic I feel.'

'Bee. I need to try to explain something to you,' I said, and she clasped her hands together, all prim and calm looking.

'The Misses Allen are really lovely people, but you mustn't let them prod your imagination with things like this.'

'You think it's not true?' she asked, frowning.

'I *know* it's not.'

She'd become excited and hopeful and I was annoyed with the Misses Allen right then – for poking the dark stick at my sister's already madness-prone imagination. I'd never been stupid enough to mention Hotel Magnificent to her for all these years, and neither should anyone else have been.

Why had the Misses Allen decided that now was the time for blurting out their loony legends – right now when thoughts of death and loss were weighing down on my sister, when she was at her most vulnerable.

Oh, Misses Allen. Honestly. How unhelpful.

It was true that some people used to *say* there was a laneway that led to an old ruined 'Hotel Magnificent' from the road but it too had become knotted and strangled with overgrowth and slowly swallowed up by the passing of time. If there had ever been a building there or a ruin, it was almost definitely long gone. And not all the stories about it were scary or frightening. Some people said that on still nights they could hear music drifting down from those heights – lovely music that soothed people's troubled lives or sparked memories of happy times that were gone, or just made people feel calm and hopeful in times of trouble and fear. But whenever people strained to listen, the sounds would disappear, and then they thought that it was something they must have imagined. Some said that on stormy nights other sounds could be heard from there too: the voices of dead loved ones; old stories, long-forgotten; the names of living people, spoken by the dead. And I guess I understand how a legend such as that might linger in the heads of people who wanted something to believe in.

Anyway, the point was, I didn't want these kinds of thoughts in my little sister's already active imagination. All I wanted was for her to be safe and happy and not sad and not full of desperate longing.

I sat on the grass with Bee and tried to think of more practical ways to cheer her up, such as pointing out that the sun had begun to shine again. Janine came to the door, shielding her eyes.

'Come on in. Everyone's going to be so happy to see you back. Aunt Lucy has made scones. They're in the oven. They're almost ready.'

'Who is Aunt Lucy to barge her way into our house and make scones in our kitchen? Whoever said we even wanted scones? Isn't there plenty of other stuff for everyone to eat?' asked Bee.

We struggled to our feet. I grabbed my bicycle.

'Don't you think that's a pretty strange thing to do?' she continued. 'I mean, making scones in someone else's house?'

'Oh, come on,' I said to her. 'She's only trying to help. Maybe it would be a good idea to give her a chance.'

I decided not to dwell on it any further. I was too worried about Bee, if I was honest, to overthink the actions of a long-lost relative who had burst uninvited into our lives.

It was a cruel thing about life: people you really wanted sometimes disappeared, and people you didn't want at all sometimes arrived, and if anyone thought about that for too long, they'd go mental. When we got back inside, Uncle Freddy hugged Bee for ages, bringing again such fresh memories of Granddad that I had to sit in the bathroom for a few minutes with the door locked.

There was something that basically terrified me about the way Bee's eyes had looked when she'd spoken about Hotel Magnificent, and about the way her whole body trembled with hope.

'If Uncle Freddy knew you were even *thinking* about climbing up behind Dillon's Park, he'd have a full-blown massive heart attack,' I explained to her when I emerged from the bathroom in response to her hammering on the door.

'Gosh, we'd be in a right old pickle then!' she exclaimed.

'Correct. So no more discussion about imaginary, ruined places on the top of dangerous cliffs then,' I said as we headed into the kitchen for the scones.

'My lips are utterly sealed,' she replied, which somehow did not reassure me at all.

*

So we poured out tea and people stood around, munching on the fresh scones, which even Bee had to admit were kind of delicious.

'There's someone at the door for you,' said Uncle Freddy suddenly with an illogical-looking smile on his face.

My mouth was still full. I hadn't put a single drop of make-up on and, after the unexpected bike ride to town, my hair was all over the place. I peered out of the side window.

It was Chris Crosby. At the door. Of my house.

I spoke to him through the letter box. 'Listen,' I said, 'could you come back in like twenty minutes or so? There are just a couple of things I have to do.'

'Yeah, OK,' he said and I breathed a massive sigh of relief and dashed upstairs to do my face. When I came down again, Bee was shaking her head. 'Gracie, honestly, what are you doing?' she asked.

'Nothing,' I told her.

'I meant to come earlier,' Chris said when he'd come back and when I'd finally let him see me.

'Yeah no problem, thanks,' I said, suddenly feeling strange and wobbly. 'Do you want to come in?'

'Do you want me to?'

'If you'd like,' I said.

'How are you feeling?' he asked, but I wasn't able to tell him. I couldn't explain how impossible it was to think of Granddad Patrick being gone for ever. How hard it was to see Bee so tormented and desperate, and to watch Uncle Freddy doing his best to keep it all together. And I couldn't talk to him about Aunt Lucy's sudden arrival because somehow that felt weird and complicated too.

Instead I offered him food, and he went round shaking everyone's hands and telling people who he was. We sat at the kitchen table and Chris picked up one of the cupcakes with yellow buttercream and red chocolate hearts that the Misses Allen had made and said, 'Mmm. Excellent. Have one too.'

'Not hungry,' I replied.

I started talking to him then about what a great guy my grandfather had been and how much we were going to miss him and I did my best not to let my voice tremble but a couple of times I couldn't help it.

'He was really old though,' said Chris, finishing the last of the cake and reaching for another. 'I mean, he was going to have to die sooner or later, wasn't he?'

And even though Chris Crosby was completely amazing, I realised then that in some ways, he was like everyone else. He didn't understand that age and sadness have nothing to do with each other.

I forgave him though because, you know . . . Gorgeous face. Beautiful eyes. Perfect hair.

After Chris left, I remembered that I'd stuffed Scully's card into my pocket so I pulled it out and opened it.

On the outside was a picture of the ace of hearts.

And in it were words of love for Granddad – words of kindness and memory – that Scully had not been able say out loud.

Everyone had gone home and Bee and I were in bed by the time the argument between Uncle Freddy and Aunt Lucy started. At first I could only hear the change in their voices, and I didn't know exactly what they were arguing about, but then I realised it was about us. He shouted our names and she shouted something about the house and then Uncle Freddy said:

'THE GIRLS ARE FINE. I'M TAKING GOOD CARE OF THEM, AND FRANKLY THEIR WELFARE IS NONE OF YOUR BUSINESS.'

The next day she wasn't there. Uncle Freddy told us she'd moved to the Westbourne, which was a real hotel.

'She thinks I'm a bully,' he mumbled and Bee reached over to hold his hand.

'How long do you think she's going to hang around for?' I asked.

'God knows,' he said, the crease at the top of his nose deepening by the second.

NINE

I n the days after Granddad's funeral, neither of us had ever seen Uncle Freddy do so much cleaning. Aunt Lucy moving to the Westbourne didn't take any pressure off. In fact it made him kind of worse.

From then on, every time she rang to say she was on her way, Uncle Freddy would get into a panic, pulling out the battered hoover from under the stairs. It wasn't that easy to keep our house in great order, and Uncle Freddy still hadn't paid the bin charges, so now there were eleven black bags piled up along the side wall of our house. I wasn't too happy about letting Bee play there. The smell. All the little flies. But since Aunt Lucy had swooped back into his life, Uncle Freddy had begun to do his best to get the place in shape.

He never usually shouted, but when Aunt Lucy was on her way, roaring at us became a practically compulsory part of the preparation, and so did running downstairs and then running upstairs again very quickly, and putting up new pictures on the wall and clearing out cupboards and throwing away anything from the fridge that even looked as if it was approaching its sell-by date.

I tried to help by cooking stuff. Stuff that I thought Aunt Lucy might like. I did my special Pavlova for her, plopping fresh, fat, shiny cherries on top. I got very good at whipping the cream up exactly the right amount – puffy and full.

Aunt Lucy hated if our clothes were crushed, and she was always going on about the house – how it was very run-down, how it needed to be brightened up, that there were dark corners and spaces full of clutter in terrible need of a makeover.

And even when she wasn't actually in the house, she was in our conversations and our thoughts and in Uncle Freddy's anxious looks.

It wasn't all bad, though. We learned. We got a bit better about ironing our clothes and we developed the habit of pulling fresh flowers from the hedgerows at the bottom of the street so there were always some on the windowsill in the downstairs hall. There were feelings of ceremony and officialdom about her visits. I always felt I had to stand there when she came, and it was only right to be nice, to smile and to welcome her in.

I'd never noticed much at all about our house until Aunt Lucy started to criticise it, and then suddenly lots of blemished details began to draw me towards them and instead of being invisible, they became the only things I could see. Like how our front door was a bit buckled and had gouged a semicircle on the wooden floor in the hall. How Uncle Freddy had repaired our kitchen table, salvaged from the dump on the outskirts of the village, and how its wood was warped and cracked and pitted so that when you put bowls down, they leaned ever so slightly to one side, and the cups and saucers wobbled and clinked.

No matter how much we tried to coach and persuade her though, there seemed to be nothing we could do to convince Bee to be polite. Most of the time she wouldn't even look at Aunt Lucy and she definitely wouldn't answer any of her questions or do a single thing to help with the visits, which meant that I had to overcompensate by smiling my face off and pressing food on Aunt Lucy and doing my absolute best to make sure Bee didn't get carried away with animus. It was a terrible strain. And even though Uncle Freddy's nose crease had grown so deep and furrowed it was practically a permanent fixture on his face, you could see he was doing his best too.

Bee would get up earlier than all of us and we'd sometimes find her standing behind our front door peering through the peephole. When we asked her why, she said she was 'making sure no selfishness comes this way,' and it didn't take a psychic to know who she was talking about.

*

At school, Chris's friends in the top group barely mentioned the funeral when I got back, and within a couple of weeks, everyone seemed to have forgotten that my granddad had ever even existed. By then nobody could talk about anything except the ski trip – asking each other how many pairs of leggings they were bringing and whether they were buying new sunglasses and other similar globally critical issues of the season.

'Has everyone checked their passports are in date?' Ingrid asked the group as I studied my fingers.

'Are you coming to Trabolgan for some practice?' Norm added.

'Yeah, Gracie, you need to get your skillage up in advance of the real thing,' said Jack.

Eva had painted her nails white with little flecks of silver 'to go with the snow'.

And Jack said, 'Hey, Gracie, it's great to see your name on the list.'

'What list?' I said, blinking.

'The ski trip list,' Chris butted in. 'You need to send Mr Sanders your passport details. Oh and, by the way, you owe me two hundred and fifty.'

'I owe you what?'

'Yeah, I paid your deposit. You're welcome.'

'Chris, what the . . . ?'

'Em, stop looking so cranky about it. I saved your skin. The deadline closed while you were off. Mr Sanders said there could be no exceptions.

'I know, but I didn't know you were going to pay it. You never said . . .'

'Gracie, the clock was ticking. You'd have missed the list otherwise.'

Nobody could have ever known how cold and panicked I felt right then. I'd pretended I was going, and then he'd paid the bloody deposit and now I owed it to him and I'd no idea if Uncle Freddy had the money to pay him back.

'OK then, thanks,' was all I said, rubbing the palms of my hands on my skirt.

When I got home the dishes were still in the sink and so I began clattering the pots and pans around the kitchen. 'Never wash up angry,' Bee said, but I said it was none of her business what mood I was in when I did the washing up, and if she wasn't going to help me then she should go somewhere else. I didn't hear Aunt Lucy coming through the front door.

Louie had totally changed his mind about her, welcoming her like a beloved long-lost hero, so excited and happy to see her that he fell over from the force of his own wagging tail.

After managing to calm Louie's new-found and exaggerated affection, Aunt Lucy sat down and put her hands flat on the table. The way she did it made me stop what I was doing, I wasn't sure why.

'What's wrong, Gracie?' was all she said.

It wasn't as if I knew her properly. And up till then, it wasn't as if I was completely sure she was as nice as I wanted her to be. It was just that she asked this simple question that nobody had asked me, and right then I realised I'd been waiting to tell someone – I needed to explain what was wrong, and so halfway through the washing up, standing in the kitchen with Aunt Lucy sitting at the table, I did.

I told her about Uncle Freddy being in this terrible dark mood and us having no money, and how sad I felt about Granddad and how much I missed him, and how worried I felt about Bee and all these delusions she had, and how for some reason I didn't feel I could tell anyone about any of these things. And about Chris who was officially my boyfriend, and all my new fragile friendships. And about the skiing trip that I wasn't going on even though I owed Chris a load of money for the deposit that he'd paid while I was out of school.

And it all came out in a big tumble-rush of sorrow and anger.

'Look, I'm sorry. I feel selfish talking about this, especially now. I probably shouldn't have told you any of it.'

'Why do you think that?' asked Aunt Lucy.

'Well, it's not Uncle Freddy's fault that I can't go, and besides it's expensive and it isn't just the flights and accommodation, it's also the gear and everything you need to buy and the stuff you need to rent while you're there, and I can't expect him to pay for all that. And I feel kind of bad saying any of this to you. I mean, I've only just met you, and it's not really your concern.'

I could see then, a kind of softness in Aunt Lucy's face. She stood and then she came over to the sink beside me, very close.

'Oh but, Grace, you mustn't for a single second feel bad about saying these things to me. This is exactly what I am here for. I'm so pleased you've shared it. I'm your aunt! If you can't tell me, then who can you tell?'

And she was right. Uncle Freddy was lovely, but so many things were forbidden, and so many things seemed impossible, and I began to feel that maybe Aunt Lucy might change that, somehow.

'There are things that need to be said! Issues that must be discussed!' Aunt Lucy declared the following Saturday. Uncle Freddy made high-eyebrowed faces at us as Aunt Lucy's voice filled the room, rising from the loudspeaker of his phone on the kitchen counter.

'I want you all to come to the Westbourne tomorrow. We'll have afternoon tea. It's the perfect kind of place for a civilised discussion and the sandwiches are delicious.'

Bee began to jump up and down, gesticulating and shaking her head.

'Are you sure?' shouted Uncle Freddy from the sink. 'Wouldn't you prefer to come over?'

I grabbed Bee and jostled her into the hallway in case she might say something hostile and inappropriate. We lurked there though, and we could still hear Aunt Lucy's voice, unperturbed and confident, booming from the phone.

'Look, Fred, to be totally honest, I think neutral territory might be a good idea right now. I want to keep things civil, Fred. Civil and polite and decent, just like they'd have wanted.'

I didn't know what she meant but it was difficult to argue with Aunt Lucy. She told us all to be there the next day. Three o'clock. In the mezzanine. 'It's sort of posh,' is what she said.

'What's that supposed to mean?' asked Uncle Freddy.

'You know, dress nicely,' she replied, and then Uncle Freddy went on about how insulting it was to be instructed to do something like that and that we were always perfectly well dressed, and what was she implying. Aunt Lucy's voice rose out of Uncle Freddy's phone saying she never meant to insult anyone and all she wanted was for us all to be talking and how she was looking forward to seeing us.

And I wished I didn't have to think about the tension between Uncle Freddy and Aunt Lucy. And I wished I didn't have to think about how sad we felt about Granddad Patrick being gone. But some thoughts couldn't be banished, however much I wanted them to be.

103

TEN

Uncle Freddy and I tried our best to brush Bee's hair but she squirmed and wriggled away from us.

'The Westbourne has soft sofas,' I told her. 'It's like sitting on clouds. And roasted peanuts on all the tables, in silver bowls.'

We headed to the Dart. We walked up Nassau Street. It started to rain. Uncle Freddy dived into the bookshop to buy an umbrella. They had none left.

'Doesn't matter,' he said. 'Sure we're nearly there.' And it didn't take us long to run the rest of the way up towards the big, rotating doors of the Westbourne.

A man in a suit and a top hat said, 'Can I help you?'

'We're meeting our Aunt Lucy upstairs. She's not very nice but there are soft sofas and peanuts. In silver bowls,' said Bee.

'Right,' he said with a face like a rock, looking us up and down, 'well, if you'd like to freshen up, the bathrooms are to the left at the top.' He pointed a white gloved finger at the blanched steps in front of us, their bannister woven with twinkling lights, but Uncle Freddy said unless someone was literally dying for a pee we'd better get going to the mezzanine. We didn't want Aunt Lucy to be kept waiting, and by his calculations we were already approximately forty-five seconds late.

She was wearing a white dress and golden shoes.

'Hello, girls,' she said, leaning forward.

'Can I eat the peanuts?' Bee asked.

'I wish you'd look me in the face when you're talking to me, Bee,' said Aunt Lucy, but Bee kept on staring very intensely at the floor.

'I need to go to the toilet,' said Bee.

'Well, probably better not to have peanuts then, not until after you've been, and after your Uncle Fred and I have had a chance to talk.'

So Bee and I headed off to the loo.

'What does Uncle Freddy want to talk about to that woman?' Bee asked, pumping masses of hand cream out of a dispenser with a golden nozzle.

'She's not "that woman", she's your aunt,' I replied.

'Well I think she's mean.'

'No, she's not.'

'She is. I am able to smell it just like Louie did at first,' said Bee.

'Right, so that's another thing I hope you don't ever tell anyone.'

'What?'

'That you can smell meanness.'

'Why not? It's terribly unpleasant.'

When we got back to the table the tea had arrived. On the white-clothed table was a rack of food in three tiers that were connected by a silver rod: tiny sandwiches and scones and small dots of chocolate in frilly pink cases.

'You may take two of everything,' Aunt Lucy said. 'Bottom to top,' she instructed. 'Savoury before sweet.'

Uncle Freddy's leg shuddered nervously, which was a thing it never did.

We munched away and Bee sat pressed up close to me as we tried make sense of the conversation.

'Fred, I have entitlements, and you can't deprive me of them.'

'I'm not trying to deprive you of anything,' said Uncle Freddy, 'it's you. You are the one who deprived yourself these last five years.'

'Yes, well, I don't even know what that means,' she said, pouring the tea into delicate, shiny-rimmed cups. 'Anyway, you should know, in case it's not clear, that I am only staying in this hotel out of the goodness of my heart.'

'What goodness? What heart?' asked Uncle Freddy, cracking his knuckles.

'I'm not even going to dignify that with an answer,' she said. 'I care very deeply, Fred. Everyone has a right to their family. You can't blank it out, however much you try.'

Bee got up again then for no obvious reason, and dashed across the room.

Uncle Freddy clenched his teeth and swiped his hand through his hair.

'Gracie, go get her, will you?'

So I went off to track her down, a thing I'd probably spend my whole life doing.

When we got back to the sofas again, there were two shiny gift bags on the table.

'What are these?' asked Bee.

'They're gifts, from me,' Aunt Lucy announced.

'For us?' said Bee, her face pale with a kind of shock.

'Yes, for you,' Aunt Lucy smiled. And we both pulled out the tissue paper and lifted up small rectangular boxes and began to peel the violet paper away from what was underneath.

Aunt Lucy had bought phones for us. The newest iPhones. No one had them yet, not even Norm or Chris or Jack.

'Thank you so much,' I managed, but Bee just nodded her head and looked down at her present in silence.

'I didn't realise that you were this kind,' said Bee. 'I'm sorry.'

Uncle Freddy had stopped talking completely. I looked at him then. He had his arms folded across his chest. The big line on the bridge of his nose was like an angry scar.

'Right, now that I've won you over,' Aunt Lucy said, still smiling, 'I'd like to say something else, to you, Gracie.'

'Lucy, I'm telling you now, that's enough,' Uncle Freddy interrupted. 'You've given them the big presents – you've done your bit. You're not to talk to her about anything else, especially not . . .'

'What? What are you not to talk to me about?'

'Nothing, OK?' said Uncle Freddy and by then his face was furious enough to shut Aunt Lucy up.

'This is all terribly confusing,' said Bee.

'Yeah,' I said. 'You should let Aunt Lucy say what she was going to say.'

'She wasn't going to say anything,' said Uncle Freddy, 'and what's more, it's time for us to go home. Come on, girls.'

'But we haven't finished our cakes!' said Bee.

'Just as well,' he replied, standing up and beckoning us to get going. 'This food is far too sugary.'

We were even more baffled then. In his whole life, Uncle Freddy had never worried about what time we were supposed to go home, or about the sugar content of our meals, or anything like that.

Later that evening, while we were busy discovering the full fabulousness of our new phones, Uncle Freddy went to the pub. As it got later and later, we sat at the top of the stairs, waiting to hear him come in. As he came through the door we could hear his own phone ringing and when Uncle Freddy began shouting, it didn't take a genius to figure out that it was Aunt Lucy.

'For the last time, they don't need you barging in here and winding them up! They are fine. Enough is enough. I won't have it.'

'Goodness me, but Uncle Freddy's voice is dark like blood,' Bee whispered.

'Shut up, Bee,' I said.

'Something is happening to our poor uncle,' she said. 'Something else bad is on the horizon.'

'Bee, let's go to bed.'

I switched off the light on her doom-laden pronouncements and hopped into bed. Soon I could hear her and Louie snoring softly in unison from across the room.

Downstairs, Uncle Freddy had gone silent. I couldn't help wondering what Aunt Lucy had wanted to say to me in the Westbourne, and why he had silenced her, and what was going on between the two of them.

By the time I went to sleep, I'd sent eleven texts and received eight. One was from Aunt Lucy. 'Grace, darling. When you really want something in life, sometimes all you need to do is ask.'

'Thx,' I texted back. And the bed felt cool and smooth

against my back. I thought then about how maybe it was that simple. I was going to tell Uncle Freddy that I did want to go on the trip. I was going to ask him for the money. Maybe that was all I ever needed to do. And suddenly everything seemed easier and less complicated than it had in a while, and as I lay thinking about it my eyes adjusted to the dark, and another while after that, I could hear Uncle Freddy's solid, faithful footsteps creaking their way upstairs to bed.

ELEVEN

'I've just found out what's wrong with Uncle Freddy!' said Bee after school the next day. 'I've been suspecting it for quite some time and now I know it's true.'

'What?'

'He's lost his job in the garage.'

'Who told you that?'

'Nobody, I just know. Didn't you notice that he was home before us? Didn't you hear the dejected way he closed the front door behind him? Didn't you see how he sank into his chair? There's no mistaking it, Gracie, only one explanation: that's a man whose source of income has been unexpectedly cut off.'

'How can you possibly know all that?' I asked her.

'Attention,' she replied. 'Attention to detail.'

I didn't want her to be right. But she had that mystical face on, and later, when Uncle Freddy came in to say goodnight, he kissed each of us on the forehead and patted Louie and then stood at the door and coughed.

'Girls,' he said, 'listen, I need to tell you. Business at the garage has been very slow and, you see, I haven't exactly been fired, it's nobody's fault, but there's no work for me any more.'

'Are we going to be poor?' asked Bee tactlessly, and Uncle Freddy laughed.

'We're going to be fine,' he replied, 'and you're not to worry. I just didn't want you to hear it anywhere else. Something will come up and we'll figure things out. Isn't that what we always do? I mean, as long as we stick together, isn't that the main thing?'

And all over again, asking Uncle Freddy to pay for the trip became a complicated, impossible thing.

The next morning, Aunt Lucy rang on our way to school.

She was whispering. 'Grace, there was something else I wanted to put to you when we met, and I haven't been able to get this out of my head. I've made a decision myself now and I don't care what your uncle says, in fact I know he'd say no, but that is not the point because there are things that Barbara and Daniel would have wanted for you. And I promised that I would play my part and . . . you see . . . now's my chance.'

And she kept talking but I had stopped hearing the rest of her words because all I could hear were the names of my

112

parents banging inside my head as if someone was hitting the bottom of a saucepan with a wooden spoon.

'Barbara? Daniel? I don't know why I never asked you to talk about them. You must have known them so well.'

'Darling, of course I did, and your granddad too. We are connected in such strong ways, you and Bee and me,' she said. 'Your mother and I shared your room when we were young, just like you and Bee do now.'

Goodness. From the moment she'd arrived, I should have been spending every second of our time together asking her questions about Mum and Dad.

'All you have to do is ask me what I can do for you,' she said. 'That's all you ever have to do.'

'OK then, please come to our house today after school. Can you come? Are you free?'

And she said she was free as a bird and that there was nothing in this world that she would prefer to do and that she'd see me later.

The day seemed to take ages, and when I finally got home, she was already there. I looked at her hands and they reminded me of other hands I had once known – the ocean of darkness stirred inside me then and I felt afraid but brave too. I put my hand on her hand and an ancient sigh came from us both.

'Oh, Aunt Lucy, you can tell me all about her. You can tell me everything.'

'Gracie, sweetheart, that is what I'd love to do, it's what I've been dying to do all this time, but your Uncle Freddy is like a wall between us and I've been feeling so . . . so blocked by him and so dismissed, as if I'm interfering in your lives when all I want to do is be part of it. There is so much to tell you. There is so much I wish I could say.'

'Uncle Freddy never, ever talks about her or about dad. We've got so used to it. Anytime I try to say something, he gets silent, and in the end it is better not to mention them at all. I don't want him to be sad, and he doesn't want us to be, and now even saying their names . . . it's become sort of forbidden, at least that's how it feels. I haven't had anywhere I could go to talk about her and my dad. And now that I have you, I'm afraid.'

'What are you afraid of?'

'I'm afraid that if I take my sadness out, I won't be able to put it back. I'm afraid it will take over everything.'

The room wobbled then, and I hadn't heard him coming, but I could see the outline of Uncle Freddy at the door.

After that, there was a massive scene. It started with Uncle Freddy saying, 'I knew this would happen,' his voice raised and cold. 'Lucy, what are you doing? What are you saying? How can you come here after all this time and how can you even bloody well *dream* of making her cry?'

114

'Fred, OK, I'm sorry. It's only because . . . We were talking and she asked and I think she needs someone to—'

'Someone to WHAT? Nothing. Stop it. Leave her alone please.'

I tried to make things better. 'Uncle Freddy, it's fine – we were only having a conversation, that's all. She's not doing any harm.'

'Listen, Grace, you don't know her. She doesn't care about anyone except herself. She never bothered to turn up when everyone needed her most, and now she's here interfering with things that are none of her business.'

He turned to Aunt Lucy. There was proper rage in his eyes.

'If you are so interested in the two of them, then where have you been for the last five years? It is time for you to leave. We can get on with life, can't we, Gracie, the way we've been doing perfectly well without you, Lucy, just in case you hadn't noticed.'

'Perfectly well? Perfectly well? Fred, I don't think you've been getting on that well at all. The girls are sad and Bee has what can only be described as mental health issues, and Grace is longing to be just like her peers, and I think you need to have a long, hard look at things. You need to have a proper think about how well you're all actually doing. It's not perfect. It's not even close to perfect. It's not appropriate for eight-year-old children to pour glasses of whiskey for people and it's not right that the only game

115

Gracie gets to play is poker. It's dangerous for them to be allowed to go down to that rocky coast on their own, and to go swimming with those old women from the library. You need to think about the habits you've got them into.'

'Eh listen, Lucy, I'm not letting you twist things and cast doubt on the way I choose to care for them. You don't know anything. You can't judge us. You're not even on our side.'

'I am, don't you see? I'm not your enemy. I'm your sister. I can help. Why do you think I'm here?'

There was this grown-up pause when everyone looked at each other and then Aunt Lucy cleared her throat and I knew she was going to say something important. I just didn't know that she was going to say something great.

'Fred, please let me tell her what I want to say.'

'I've already said no,' he replied, not looking at her. 'You dragged us to your posh hotel and you gave them phones that I didn't want them to have, and there was that one thing I asked you not to do . . .'

'I don't understand,' said Aunt Lucy.

'Leave it, Lucy, please will you? Why do you have to bring it up again? Seriously. That's not helpful at all. And anyway she has talked to me about it and she's told me she's no interest. She doesn't even want to go.'

'That's where you're wrong. She's told me the truth. And the truth is there's nothing she'd like more in the world and, besides, I'd like her to go.'

116

'Oh *you'd* like her to go, would you? Well, perhaps you'd also like to remind me exactly what any of this has got to do with you.'

'I don't see why you're so against it. I mean, I'm offering to pay.'

Uncle Freddy closed his eyes for ages then, so for a second I thought he might have gone into some strange kind of spontaneous trance, but he hadn't.

'Yeah, well, thanks for that. Now she knows, so I guess there's no going back. So yeah, you win. You love that, don't you?'

'What do you mean?'

'How can I prevent it when you dangle her dreams in front of her?'

I felt a little bit guilty, but mainly I was thrilled. Aunt Lucy pulled a purse from her huge, soft, pale bag. She opened it up and plucked out all these clean, smooth, brand-new-looking fifty euro notes and put them on the table.

And then she took a floppy notebook out and opened it up with a flick of her familiar-looking fingers.

'Who will I make the cheque out to?'

Uncle Freddy looked at me and I looked back at him and there was silence again until I said, 'Two fifty to Chris Crosby and the rest to the school. Thanks. Thanks so much.'

Aunt Lucy said she'd be so happy and delighted to come

with me to pick out my gear – my helmet and goggles and sunglasses – all the things I was going to need now that I was able to go.

'Come on, Fred, say something,' she said, looking at him then.

'What do you want me to say?' he asked.

'Thank you might be nice,' she replied.

'Oh yeah, thank you. Thank you for ignoring my wishes. Thank you for doing the opposite of what I asked. Thanks for the big gesture – trust you to come here and do something like this, something that I can't possibly forbid.'

'Why would you forbid it, Fred? Why would you stop me being generous?'

'This is not generosity – this is control and this is manipulation and this is calculation.'

'What do you mean?'

'I mean, you disappear for years and we barely get an email out of you and you never come home – and then here you are throwing money at her from a height. Oh yeah, that makes everything better, doesn't it? And I'm sure it makes you feel great about yourself too, the huge, stinking help that you are. Thanks. Thanks so much, Lucy. Thanks a bloody million.'

I saw his sadness and his anger and his embarrassment. And I saw too the power that she had. I pretended I didn't see any of it. And I'm still sometimes ashamed when I think of it.

But at the time, the only thing I could think about was that I was going skiing with the top group and with Chris Crosby and I was going to be wearing great gear. I was going to take selfies with them and people were going to be jealous of me, and maybe that was a terrible reason to be glad, but I was. And mainly I was going to put skis on my feet and go flying down the side of a mountain with snow spraying out behind me and the coldness hitting my face under blue crisp skies. For ten whole days, there'd be no grief at every turn where Grandfather Patrick used to be and no Bee annoying me and no Louie and no Uncle Freddy and no ghosts and no soundless stories about my dead parents hanging in the air, wishing to be told.

TWELVE

Uncle Freddy hardly said a word to me, but I was too busy to worry about it. I had a trip to get ready for and a whole rake of shopping to do, and there wasn't a lot of time.

I didn't need him to go with me because Aunt Lucy was here and by the time we'd finished I had everything anyone could need. Red ski pants, purple goggles and a pair of sunglasses that cost so much I thought I might faint.

I deserved my place in the top group for sure now. And it was exciting to me that the sadness and weirdness stuffed into our little house didn't seem quite as sad or weird as it normally did.

A few days before I left, Bee disappeared as usual, just as tea was ready, and also as usual, I was sent to find her.

She and Louie were sitting glumly by the sea, looking out over the water.

'Are you going to come back?' she said, her chin wobbling.

'Of course I'm going to come back, silly. You know I am.'

'How can I be sure?'

'Because I'm telling you, and anyway, who doesn't come home from a school ski trip, honestly?'

'I don't know. Maybe lots of people. I don't have access to any of the statistics,' she sniffed.

'Bee, it's teatime and Uncle Freddy's in terrible enough form already without us being late. Come on.'

All the way back home Bee chatted to Louie. 'Don't worry Louie,' she said, 'Gracie will only be gone for a little while. She won't be away for ever. She's going to come back.'

'Louie is desperately worried about you getting on a plane,' she said to me that evening.

I explained to Bee for the millionth time that Louie was a dog and that he could not talk.

'Of course he can. If you thought about it for one second you'd know,' she replied with this smug voice she used, especially when she was defending her fantasies. 'I mean, think about it. How else would I have known about Uncle Freddy's job? Who do you think told me about that?'

'You said it was the way he closed the door; the way he sat in the chair?'

'Yes, it was those things too, but Louie explained it all to me in a lot more detail. Louie is a mine of information, if people would only listen. Apparently Uncle Freddy shouted at his boss. Plus, he has a bottle of whiskey hidden in the shelves of his office.'

'And Louie told you all this?'

'Yes, but that's only the start of it, Gracie. Louie's full of whole piles of wisdom that humans normally don't have access to. He's the one who told me about Pale Emily – you know, my friend who sleeps in the park? He was the one who first knew that Grandfather Patrick was dead. And he knows about Hotel Magnificent and lots of other things besides and he tells me it all, and gosh, you know, when I think about it, I'd be pretty much lost without him.'

'Bee, if you keep on saying these things and behaving in this way, your life is going to be a basic nightmare, I hope you know that.'

'What in heaven's name do you mean?' she asked.

'Oh, never mind,' I said.

'Very well, good,' she whispered, breathing in and out deeply, holding on to me for a second to steady herself. 'Let us not speak of such things again.'

And soon there was only a day left, and I wished that I was like other people, ordinary people who didn't have to worry whether their little sister was going to be OK and whether her nightmares would still haunt her in her sleep and whether there would be someone there to comfort her when she woke up.

Bee cried that night. She said that the bald lady with sunken eyes and bony hands was back, and that she was coming to get her. And as patiently as I could, I explained again about dreams and how realistic they could feel. I let her into my bed where she clung on to me as if I was a rock and as if she was a barnacle.

And I loved her so much but at the same time – I couldn't pretend that part of me wasn't happy to leave her behind. All the madness of her longing. All the darkness of her fear.

It turned out I was pretty much a natural skier and that I could make people laugh, even very cool people like Norm and Jack and Ingrid, and it turned out that I looked really good in red ski pants and that I could move from the training slopes to the real ones sooner than lots of other people were able to, and it is pretty good to discover all those things about yourself.

'Here's to all of us,' Norm said in front of the cabin's roaring fire and we clinked our mugs of cocoa together and even though my muscles were sore and tired, I couldn't wait to get out on the snow again.

'Who'd have thought you'd be the one to catch on so fast? You're practically an expert,' said Ingrid.

And I said, 'Ah well, I don't know about that.' What I did know was that for those few days, there was nowhere else I'd rather have been. I hardly even thought about Bee.

On the last day, Chris and I dared each other to do the high slope. The trainer said we were ready. I went first and it didn't hurt when I fell over and tumbled in a snowy haze. Chris came to get me and he kneeled down beside me and then lay in the snow next to me and kissed me on the mouth for like twenty seconds. It was funny how no one asked why we'd stayed lying in the cold for so long and not having to explain made me glad and sorry at the same time.

On the plane home I sat in the middle of the crowd. We all made a vow to stick together for ever.

'You know what made the whole trip?' said Ingrid.

'What?'

'The fact that you came.'

'Yeah,' said Norm. 'It wouldn't have been the same without you.'

Everybody agreed.

I kept thinking of all the things I'd have missed if I hadn't gone, and I remembered again the blessing of Aunt Lucy arriving back in our lives when she did, and I hoped that everything between her and Uncle Freddy had calmed down while I'd been gone and that Bee was OK.

*

Bee and Louie and Uncle Freddy were in the garden. Bee was dressed in her fairy outfit with glitter on her shoes and on her cheeks. A tiara sat crookedly on Louie's head. She knelt down in front of me and put her arms around my knees and stayed like that for ages.

'Never go away again, promise me,' she said as Louie jumped up and licked both our faces.

'So much has happened. I have so much news!' She said I should be very excited, even though I wasn't.

'I have a best friend now.'

'Well, that's great,' I said.

'Yeah, I know. Give you one guess what her name is?'

'What?' I said, hoping she wasn't going to say Pale Emily.

'Wait for it . . . Wait for it . . . KATY CROSBY!'

'Katy Crosby?' I repeated. Something cold began to rumble around inside me.

'I know! Fantastic, isn't it? I can tell her anything and she listens to me and she believes everything I say, the things that nobody wants me to talk about.' She spun around in a gleeful whirl.

I'd kind of forgotten that Chris even had a sister.

I thought about all the things Bee had probably said to her already: claiming that the local library was haunted; that there was an old hotel with dead people walking around in it; that there was an invisible girl called Pale Emily in Dillon's Park; that Louie could speak to her.

It felt as if something was twisting in my head. Bee's

125

secrets would be the end of us. Now she was friends with Chris's sister and no one knew how long *that* had been going on and I thought for a second that I was probably going to cry.

It wasn't her only news. When she finally stopped hugging me, she whispered about how she'd got into 'a little bit of trouble' at school.

'What do you mean by that?' I asked, with a sinking heart.

'I was accused of vandalism, but I'm not guilty.'

Bee had been missing me. She escaped from the junior school across the pitches and through the fence. Someone had seen her hanging around and there was something scrawled on the dented metal door of my locker in permanent marker: *GO TO HOTEL MAGNIFICENT*. Nobody knew what it meant. One of the third years had brought her back to her side of the fence.

She admitted to escaping from school but she denied she'd written anything on my locker, even though everyone knew it was her.

Uncle Freddy had had to go in to discuss it with Mrs Collins. And Bee had gone with him.

'So what happened then?' I asked as she jumped around again in her gossamer skirt, her wings flapping on her back, her shoes twinkling in the last of the sunshine.

'Oh, Gracie, I thought I was in terrible trouble, but in the end it was a perfectly nice meeting. Well, I mean, it wasn't at first, the way Mrs Collins sat silently at one side of a massive desk and the way she'd arranged two chairs on the other side and the awfully formal way she invited Uncle Freddy and me to sit down. And plus, it wasn't that nice the way she stared at me and Uncle Freddy for more time than I personally thought was strictly polite, leafing very slowly through a hardback notebook that had "Student incidents" written on the cover. You can't imagine how nervous I felt for that bit.'

'No, I'm sure I haven't a clue,' I said. 'So what did she say to you?'

'All she said then was that I was a very delightful and quite lovely girl, who must be missing her sister.'

'And what did you say?'

'Nothing, I just stared at her, so amazed at how complimentary and understanding she was being when I'd been expecting something entirely different. Mrs Collins said there was nothing wrong with missing someone, but that when a pupil leaves the premises during school hours and when she defaces property with disturbing messages, it was time for her to speak to the parents.'

'Oh dear, Bee.'

'It doesn't really bother me too much. The way the world constantly refers to parents as if they are all alive. I get it. It's only because most people's parents are.'

'I'm not talking about what *she* said, I'm talking about

you. Why on earth did you write such a weird thing on my locker door?'

'This is what I keep telling everyone. It *wasn't* me.

'Who did it, then?'

'Can't you guess?'

I couldn't.

'Pale Emily of course! It's so sad for her. Scrawling out a message on your locker door is the only way she can get you to notice her. She's tried everything else but it appears there is no other medium at her disposal, poor thing. So anyway, the whole thing got all mixed up and everyone thought I was the culprit. Isn't it so ridiculous? Mrs Collins says it's very disconcerting. She says that we need to put our heads together to see what can be done. She thinks I've made up Pale Emily inside my head. She thinks I'm talking about a not real person. She doesn't realise that Pale Emily is alive.'

I lifted my eyebrows and let out a long breath.

Of course this was waiting to happen, I thought. Bee's delusions were bound to leak and spill and spread into other parts of her life. Nobody was going to keep a lid on stuff like that and it was probably going to get worse.

'Look, we're going to have to help Bee figure a few things out,' said Uncle Freddy the next day. 'I had a good talk with Mrs Collins, and she was excellent. She says that there are some quite simple, useful strategies that we might try, to keep Bee's feet a bit more firmly on the ground.'

'Good luck with that,' I replied.

Uncle Freddy agreed it was probably wise to have Bee assessed – by proper doctors who knew what they were talking about and who could help Bee to stop being so weird.

Bee claimed to be excited at the prospect, but when the time came, she wasn't that impressed at all.

'He had jeans on and his jumper was bobbly. He didn't have a stethoscope or a white coat. And he had no little black rod with a light at the end of it for looking in my eyes. I think there's quite a good chance he isn't a doctor at all,' she claimed.

Whether he was a doctor or not, he told Uncle Freddy what was wrong with Bee. She had 'circumstantially induced mental stress'. He suggested it might have had something to do with the recent death of our grandfather.

'Did you point out that her mentalness was a pre-existing condition? That Granddad's death had nothing to do with it?' I asked.

Unsurprisingly, Uncle Freddy had not pointed that out.

The doctor's advice was simple: we were absolutely not to indulge her fantasies any more because they were getting destructive. It was our job to try to get her to stop referring to them and hope that she'd forget about them.

'How much did you have to pay for him to tell you that?' I asked, pointing out that I'd been advising basically the same thing for years.

Uncle Freddy was full of resolve though, and I thought at least maybe now something would improve. The doctor suggested we get Bee to write a list of things that were real and focus on them and that eventually the things that weren't real would fade away.

We tried to explain.

'A figment? That's what you think Pale Emily is? And you want her to become extinct?'

That was it in a nutshell.

Bee was outraged.

'Pale Emily is my friend,' she insisted. 'She told me all about herself. She actually lives in Hotel Magnificent – the cave in Dillon's Park is only a stopgap for when she's stuck and she doesn't feel like climbing back up the cliff walk. She's not a figment. She says we can visit her anytime we have the energy.'

'Bee. Why do you keep on making things up? Really, why do you insist on talking like a psycho?'

'If you think I'm a psycho, you shouldn't talk to me at all. You're perfectly free to take no notice, to forget I said anything.'

'I'm constantly trying to forget, but you're making it more impossible all the time. When you keep saying crazy things, it gets harder and harder.'

We went out to the green, but it was muddy and damp and we couldn't sit down. She stood frowning at me, her lips a hard line of defiance.

'Bee, don't you see how important it is for you to stop all this about Hotel Magnificent and imaginary people and talking dogs?'

'You don't believe me. You never believe me! Everyone thinks I am mad, but I AM NOT!'

Bee stamped her foot and the ground squelched and droplets of mud flew into the air and some of them landed on my face.

I closed my eyes and did my best to wipe the mud splatter away. There wasn't much point in getting angry or sad. I tried to keep my voice low and steady and I put my hands on Bee's cheeks so she wouldn't look away – so she would listen to me.

'Bee, I need you to try to understand. Uncle Freddy is stressed out of his head. Everyone is beginning to think you have some kind of awful, trauma-related condition, so you've got to try to keep it together right now. Just put a lid on all this imaginary crap. We are getting over Grandfather Patrick's death, and we're getting used to Aunt Lucy's arrival, and we're feeling a little shaky. I know we are. And right now, there is just no room for your imagination.'

'Imagination is the greatest thing in the world,' Bee replied, offended. 'That's what Grandfather Patrick himself always told us. Don't you remember?'

'Well, maybe it's true. But right at the moment, your imagination is only going to make everyone miserable. So can you try to switch it off?'

I don't know why, but for a moment I remembered the little, cheerful, happy baby she'd once been.

'Do you think you can do that for me, Beebee? There are plenty of good things that are real, and those are the things you should be focusing on now. Otherwise you'll spend your entire life in a fog of fantasy and that's not going to be any good for anyone.'

In the days after that, Bee was quiet and subdued and still I didn't know what to do about her. But at the weekend, I dug out one of her sparkly notebooks and I asked her to start what the doctor had suggested: write a list of things that mattered, of things that were important, things that were real.

She clapped her hands. 'Gracie! A list of real things! What a great idea!'

And I said, 'OK, let's go then.'

'Katy Crosby's party!' she said first, skipping around and cheering like someone who'd won the lottery.

'Katy's party? Katy's having a party?'

'Yes. I'm invited, and I need a dress.'

From the moment she told me, I thought Bee going to Katy's party was a terrible idea. I was sure something dreadful would happen – mainly that she'd do something embarrassing.

Bee was all rush and bustle, and when she got like that there was no stopping her.

'Uncle Freddy. Come on, let's go,' she said, pulling him through the front door and outside into the air.

'Let's go where?' he laughed.

'Town. To get my dress.'

'What dress?'

'The dress for Katy Crosby's party.' Bee crouched down to pluck two fistfuls of flowers from the grass. 'I am to be . . .' she threw the flowers up into the sky above her head so that they landed in her hair '. . . the actual guest of honour.'

'No, you're not,' I said, but Uncle Freddy looked at me and did this peace-making face of his which actually meant 'let Bee say whatever she likes'.

'What happened to not indulging her fantasies?' I muttered but Uncle Freddy ignored me.

'What happened to not following people round and listening to their business?' Bee replied.

'Yeah well, she already has loads of dresses. She doesn't need a new one.'

Uncle Freddy stood up from his crouching position and said, 'Come on, Gracie, be fair, think about how much you've got recently, and think about how she's only small and she has a party to go to.'

He turned back to Bee then and smiled at her.

'It's the least we can do for you, isn't it, love?'

'Exactly,' said Bee in a not particularly grateful way, and the two of them went off to town in Uncle Freddy's beat-up van and I went back into the house and sat in the kitchen, staring at the wall, until Aunt Lucy rapped on the window so loud it made me practically fall off the chair.

THIRTEEN

It was good to see her. Her face seemed even kinder still, and the atmosphere in the house suddenly felt all delicate and lovely. Probably because Uncle Freddy and Bee weren't there.

I made tea.

'You know your uncle is a very kind and generous person,' said Aunt Lucy, 'but honestly, he's the most stubborn man I've ever met.'

The next thing Aunt Lucy and I were full-on chatting about a whole lot of things. I told her all about the trip and Chris and how brilliant everything had been.

'Well, that sounds just wonderful,' Aunt Lucy said.

'Yes, and it's all thanks to you because I never would have gone without you. But now that I'm back Bee is ruining it, just like she ruins so many things.'

'How is she ruining it?'

Aunt Lucy listened as I tried to explain.

'I am considerate and I am responsible and I try my best to be mature and I'd never even think of asking him for a dress or anything else. She winds him around her finger and he does everything she asks, even when we can't afford it. I know it's not Uncle Freddy's fault – it's because he wants her to be happy. It's because he is so kind.'

'Goodness,' she said, staring out the window and looking kind of grim.

'And I think Uncle Freddy needs help, not that he would ever ask for it, but I sometimes think everything is a bit much for him. He tries his best, but he forgets important stuff like ironing and signing our homework, plus the bins outside are manky because he hasn't paid the rubbish collectors and Bee and I often have to get out of the van and push it because it doesn't start of its own accord.'

Uncle Freddy never seemed to be able to see how manipulative and annoying Bee could be.

And I was sick of her embarrassing me and showing me up, especially now that I had new friends and a brilliant boyfriend and everything.

'Gracie, I'm so glad you've told me all this,' said Aunt Lucy after I'd finished, and I was glad too. It was great to get it out of my head. It was great to have someone to tell.

Bee's new dress was the palest yellow and Uncle Freddy had also bought her these satin shoes in exactly the same colour and a long, wide, liquid-looking ribbon for her hair.

She said she was going to try it on for me to see, but when I said there was no need, Bee said of course I was right, that it must be put away until it was time. It was to hang quietly in the wardrobe and no one was to disturb it until the day of the party.

I convinced myself that all I wanted to do was to save Bee from hurt and humiliation. I was sure that no friendship was going to be able to withstand the extremes of her weirdness and a party would be exactly the environment in which she was most likely to show herself up. But the real truth was that I didn't want her in Chris's house at Chris's sister's party being all weird and Beeish in front of all of Chris's family.

And so this was what I did. I told Bee at the last minute that Katy's party had been cancelled.

And I told Chris that my sister Bee was sick and asked him to tell Katy that she wouldn't be coming to the party on Saturday.

'Pity,' he said. 'Katy will be gutted.'

'Yeah, well, also, will you please ask Katy not to mention Bee being sick? She's very upset about it. And tell her not to talk about the party when everyone's back at school next week because that would upset her too.'

'OK, sure,' said Chris, sounding sort of puzzled.

I thought I'd saved myself a truckload of awkwardness and embarrassment. I was in the middle of working on

137

her, trying to get her to improve. A big noisy party was the absolute last thing she probably needed no matter how much she was looking forward to it. I was her sister. I knew what was best for her, and it was definitely not that.

'The whole thing is cancelled?' Bee had said. 'Everything?'

'Yes.' I looked at the floor.

'The chocolate fountain and the clown and the balloons and the bouncy castle? All of it?'

'Yes, the whole thing.'

I was relieved that she seemed to be taking it pretty well. She just lay on the sofa, staring at the ceiling for a while, but she didn't cry and she didn't get angry and she didn't even seem too sad.

'These things happen,' I had explained. It wasn't Katy's fault. People got sick and nobody could do anything about it. And it was a shame all right.

'Poor Katy,' said Bee.

And even though that seemed to be that, there was something in the thinness of her voice that made me wonder whether I was doing the right thing after all.

I knew I hadn't fully thought it through, but I convinced myself that I was protecting her. I didn't rate her ability to make friends and I had zero confidence that she could behave normally in social environments. But I knew I was protecting myself too. My reputation. My good name, such as it was.

I tried to cheer her up.

'Hey, Bee, we need to work on your list, just like the doctor said.' And Bee said yes, she thought that was a good idea.

'Uncle Freddy and Aunt Lucy,' she said, 'they are real, aren't they?'

'Yes,' I said, 'yes, of course they are.'

'Well, you say *of course*, but it's not always completely obvious to me. I need to clarify. Louie is real, isn't he?' she continued.

'Yes.'

'And the Misses Allen?'

'Real, but mad,' I replied.

'And Mum and Dad, are they real?'

I had to think about that for a while myself. In the end I said, 'I think you can say that they used to be real but they're not real any more.'

'Aha, right, I get it! So you can be real and then not be! Interesting!' she said, scribbling furiously. 'And can other things be not real and then become real?'

'Yes,' I said. 'Maybe. I mean, no. I mean, I don't know.'

'Oh gosh, confusing! Can we go back to the beginning? What's the difference between real and imaginary again?'

'Bee, look: real things are people and things and events that actually happen. Imaginary things are things you make up inside your head. Nobody else can see them.'

'I imagined a cormorant on a rock this morning.'

'What?'

'He was lovely and black and slippery and he dived under the sea and then kept popping up in different places and it was a good game to try to keep spotting him from the beach very early, while all of you were sleeping.'

'Bee. Did you see him with your own eyes?'

'Yes,' she said.

'Well, then the cormorant is real, OK, and you can put it on the list.'

'But nobody else could see him because nobody else was there.'

'If someone else was there, would they have seen him?'

'I don't know. I haven't a clue, in fact,' she said. 'I guess it depends on whether they'd have looked in the same places as me.'

We spent at least half an hour debating whether or not Bee's cormorant was a real thing and which of her lists it should go on. And was there another human being on the planet, I wondered, who would ever have to have a conversation like this with anyone?

By then, I'd put Katy's party so firmly out of my head that I'd practically forgotten about it myself.

I didn't know, when we clambered into Uncle Freddy's van to go to the shops, that he was going to take the shortcut. I didn't even notice that we were passing the corner of Sorrento Road and Coliemore. And by the time I realised, it was too late.

So we were in Uncle Freddy's rusty van and Bee was hanging out of the rolled-down window. I did my best to stop her, but when Bee decided she wanted to look at something there really was nothing anyone could do.

'Uncle Freddy, stop the car. Just stop for a sec,' she said.

'Why? What?'

'I need to check something.'

The way she spoke was so strong and certain that Uncle Freddy did stop, before he'd had a chance to ask himself whether or not it was ever wise to obey any of Bee's random instructions.

'What the . . . ? Where are you . . . ?' he shouted after her as she slid open the door with a *whoosh*, and hopped out.

And then before I could even unbuckle my seat belt she did her wild-legged tumbling run with her arms and legs flinging themselves out from her body in all different directions.

'Go after her, Gracie, please,' sighed Uncle Freddy.

Chris and Katy's house looked the same as it always did – neat grass and sandstone wall and gleaming black gates and shiny front door – but that day there was something different. Two shadows floated and bumped softly against each other as Bee stood still at the gate – black and white and enormous and high above us. A big, arched sign hung over Katy's front door. '*THE PARTY IS HERE*'.

'Katy's having the party,' she said to me, quiet and stunned, with her teeth clamped together. 'It hasn't been cancelled. Her parents didn't change their minds. Katy's not sick at all. It was all a big lie. My yellow dress is hanging in the cupboard. They're having the party without me.'

A rush of coldness filled me up and I could almost see the truth, like a stone, jagged and heavy, sinking into her brain, and it kind of felt as if I didn't already know, as if this was as shocking to me as it was to her. I had to get us away from there then – as quickly as I could.

I ran and she ran after me, and we both climbed quietly back into the van.

'What the heck is going on, girls?' asked Uncle Freddy.

We told him nothing was.

Uncle Freddy said, 'We're supposed to be getting the groceries.'

And Bee said, 'Please, just take us home,' and put her head in her hands. Her cries were soft and deep and bleak enough to break our hearts.

Bee's anguish only got worse, and soon she was saying all the things that no one was supposed to say.

'Why do we have no parents, and why did Grandfather have to die and why did Aunt Lucy come back and ruin everything, and how come there is no one here to help us, and why did Katy disinvite me from her party? What did I do?'

At home, Bee kept crying and crying and crying, and it was obvious that Uncle Freddy didn't know how to handle it. I texted Aunt Lucy about the situation, because there was something about Bee then that I didn't recognise and I was scared of it. I put my arms around her. I needed her to get back to being the way she usually was.

'One day I won't be able to hug you like this,' she said.

'Why not?'

'Because you'll be dead, or I will, or we'll both be.'

And I didn't know what to say to her, and I kept thinking it was me. It was my fault that she was feeling these things and thinking these thoughts.

And then Aunt Lucy arrived and I heard Uncle Freddy say, 'Listen, Lucy, Bee's had a bit of a disappointment and I'm trying to cope with a situation here, so the timing is not great. Can you call back later?' But Aunt Lucy didn't sound as if she had any intention of calling back later – she sounded as if she was going to stay exactly where she was – and soon she was saying horrible things too.

'This was all bound to come to a head, I hope you realise that, Fred. This is Bee's grief, bottled up and strangled in silence for too long.'

I butted in then: 'What? What are you talking about?'

And Uncle Freddy told me to go upstairs and start my homework, even though it was a Saturday and I didn't have any. I heard him tell Aunt Lucy, 'They were both absolutely FINE until you came along and destabilised everything.

They were doing grand. I will not have you make them think about things they don't need to think about or feel things they do not feel. I will not let you take away their cheerful souls.'

'Cheerful? What do you mean cheerful? Bee is grieving and crying and she doesn't even know why.'

'It's because of the party, you idiots,' I said to myself as I lay on the bedroom floor beside my sister whose tears had dried but who was still gulping with little after-sobs, like a ticking clock.

'It's only since you arrived that the problems started. You can't come here and tell them how to be, or rake up things that should not be raked up. I will not allow it,' went on Uncle Freddy, his words coming out in one big, long breath.

'You? You won't *allow* it. And how arrogant is that? They're my nieces too. I mean, who are you to decide things like that?'

'Who am I? Who am *I*? Only the person who's been here for them, day after day, for all the small things, all the important things, all the big things since . . . since . . . since . . .'

'Say it, Freddy. Since she died. Since they both died. Why can't you say it?'

'God almighty, Lucy, be quiet, will you – the girls are directly overhead. They'll hear.'

'Maybe they should hear – maybe even the vaguest

144

bloody reference to their parents' deaths shouldn't be banned – because, face it, that is what you have done. Fred, come on. It's really bad. Bee and Gracie are afraid to mention their own mother's name. I know for a fact that's not healthy.'

'Oh and you're the fountain of all knowledge, are you? You, who we haven't seen in almost a decade.'

'Stop exaggerating, Fred. It's five years.'

'Oh, sorry, yeah, of course it's only been five years. That makes everything OK then, does it? Lucy, she asked you to be there for the girls. It was the one thing she asked you.'

'I'm here now, aren't I?'

'Well, we don't need you. It's too late. You're the human proof that children can't wait for ever for someone to rock up. I'm their person now. Get over it. Go off and get on with your significant life, the one that's been too important to leave till now. The only reason you're here now is to keep an eye on me. You thought I wasn't good enough for the girls, that I would see them wrong.'

'Oh yeah, and I don't have a point? What about losing your job and drinking at work? Is that appropriate, really, for the guardian of children? What about all that?'

'I don't consider that to be any of your business. They haven't turned out too bad. I might have my issues, but I take care of those girls. They're not spoilt or cosseted. Look at them – they're perfect. And what's more, they know their own minds, they are kind and they don't judge people.

145

Did you hear that? They don't judge anyone – they're not judgemental. Ha – easy to see they didn't get that from you.'

'Fred. You can't talk to me like this. They're just as much mine as they are yours!' said Aunt Lucy.

'Mine? Yours? They're not handbags. They're human beings,' said Uncle Freddy. 'HUMAN BEINGS!'

It went on for ages. Bee put her hands over her ears.

'Fred, the house is a mess. The girls are unhappy. You don't have the wherewithal to take care of them properly.'

We could hear a rustle of papers and then Uncle Freddy asking Aunt Lucy what it was, and her saying that this was a letter from a lawyer, and the letter said that our house was her house too and nobody could send her away, and nobody could stop her from being here. We heard her say that she had made a decision and the decision was that she was moving in to help with the girls. She told Uncle Freddy that if he thought about it for even a second he'd realise this was the right thing for everyone. Next thing, there was the creaking of floorboards and a small knock on the door of our room and then the swish of it opening and even though I didn't look up we knew he was there. His voice had grown husky from all the shouting.

'Uncle Freddy, will you please do your best not to roar at Aunt Lucy any more? Bee's upset enough as it is.'

'Bee,' he said 'I know it doesn't feel like this now, but I promise you'll get over this. You'll bounce back. Soon you'll forget all about it.'

'Do you really think she will?' I replied, my voice dead and flat and jaded.

'Gracie, please stop, not now. I've had enough. I don't want to have to deal with any more drama. I've enough going on with Lucy doing my head in downstairs.'

Now it was my turn to be angry.

'Uncle Freddy, what has happened to you? I am *glad* Aunt Lucy has come back.'

'You don't understand,' he said tiredly and without much fight left in him as far as I could see.

'Maybe not, but there are lots of things I do understand. Such as, if it had been up to you, I'd have never got to go skiing; such as, if Granddad Patrick were still alive, you'd never have the nerve to fight with Aunt Lucy the way you've been doing. But you've turned into a bully, in front of my eyes.'

'Gracie, I—'

'And if my parents were still alive, I wouldn't have been forced to live with you in the first place.'

I expected Uncle Freddy to tell me to stop being such a horrible brat. I wanted him to say something that would make me stop shouting at him. I wanted him to explain that all he'd ever done was his best for me and Bee, but he didn't do anything like that. He just lowered himself down on my bed and sat looking at the wall, nodding his head, saying nothing.

It was terrible.

But the worst of all was Bee, because now she was hiding under her duvet, all tightly curled up in a ball, sobbing and sobbing and sobbing, and we couldn't get her out and we couldn't calm her down.

Uncle Fred said he had to go out for a while. 'I don't know what to say. I don't know what to do,' he said before clicking the door shut.

I tried to quieten my misshapen thoughts. And I did my best to imagine what Granddad Patrick would have said to us in a situation like this.

'Granddad,' I whispered in despair and desperation, even though I knew he was dead. 'Granddad, help me. You'd know what to do.' But apart from Bee's hiccupy sobs, there was only silence.

FOURTEEN

I couldn't bear to stay inside the house, but there was nowhere to go. In the end, it was why I went out to the shed. I reckoned that if I sat in there for a while I might be able to get my thoughts together, to calm down. I couldn't stand being so close to Bee's feelings, so awful and anguished that they seemed to shake the house, and I didn't want to think of her all curled up in bed with nobody being able to comfort her. But most of all I couldn't bear that it was all my fault.

I headed through the kitchen, out into the garden and down towards the shed. The normally padlocked door was swinging open. I walked inside. Even in the woody darkness I could see something. Something big. Something that wasn't usually there.

It was a package wrapped in brown paper. I put my hand on it and it crinkled with mysterious promise. There was an envelope stuck to the front.

'*For Bee,*' it said. I'd known that handwriting for most of my life.

I ran back into the house and sprinted up the stairs.

'Bee?' I said.

No reply.

'Listen, Bee, guess what? There is a massive package. It's in the shed. Someone has left it there. It's got your name on it.'

When you tell someone there's a present in the shed for them it doesn't take long for them to cheer up enough to go down and check it out.

Bee scrambled out of bed. Apart from bare feet, she was still fully dressed. I didn't tell her to put on her shoes, or coat, though normally I would have. We sneaked downstairs, Bee's bare feet pattering across the kitchen behind me, and out through the back door. She ran after me down the garden path, which was cold and knobbly underfoot. For a moment I saw shadows of what seemed like people, standing in the doorway of the shed, but as we got closer, the shadows were gone. Bee moved in slow motion, reaching for the card, pulling it from the package, opening it and unfolding it. Her hands were trembling and her eyes were glossy and her voice quivered as she read:

'*BEE. You are resourceful and you are resilient and you must be the captain of your own adventures. This should contain everything you need. With great love from your Grandfather Patrick.*'

She folded the card in half and shoved it into her pocket.

'Help me,' she said, excited and solemn, dragging the back of her hand across her face. Together we began to unwrap.

The paper was tight as a drum and there was old-fashioned string tying it all together. We were wordless and careful. It felt important.

'I know what it is,' said Bee. 'Look. Look what Grandfather Patrick has given us. Oh, Gracie, look.'

FIFTEEN

It was a tent. Beautiful. Shiny. Pale blue. There were two sleeping bags all rolled up and ready in their own drawstring bags. There was a box filled with leaden weights and a rainbow of spinners and hooks and spools of fishing string. And there were two gleaming, shiny fishing rods with sturdy handles and glistening black reels. And a torch.

If a heart could lift and sink at the same time, then that was what mine did right then, because I already knew. I knew what I was going to have to do next.

I was going to have to take Bee to Dillon's Park. We were going to have to pitch the tent together, and scramble down to the water and climb up to Seaweed Rock, and we were going to have to try to catch some fish, and I was going to have to light a fire – and I didn't think she would wait another moment.

'He's given me a gift from beyond the grave! It's as if

he's not even dead!' said Bee, jumping up and down and clapping her hands. 'Thank you, Grandfather Patrick, you're my absolute hero!'

I didn't even bother discussing it. I just wrote a note for Uncle Freddy and left it in the kitchen. '*Granddad left tent in shed for Bee. Just found it. Have taken her to camp in Dillon's Park. It will cheer her up. Will be fine. We'll pitch up for a couple of hours and I'll take her fishing, and it will make her happy again. Don't worry, we'll be fine. Love G x.*'

The tent had a bag with straps. It was easy to carry. Bee skipped along beside me and all the sadness and anger lifted out of her, floating away, and the happy girl was back and that, I supposed, was the main thing.

We trekked through the trees behind the tall wall, past the green patch where we used to play football in the summer and up the back hill to the very furthest corner, close to the broken gap that led to the wild cliff walk. Louie came too, which was probably what saved us in the end. The tent didn't take very long to pitch, and we unrolled the sleeping bags and struggled into them and then squirmed around, laughing like we hadn't laughed in ages. We got out again and lit a bonfire and Bee's face looked a little scary in the strange late afternoon light that danced and flashed around her.

'We are adventurers; we are pioneers. No more narrow, airless moments thinking about mean girls who disinvite people from their parties!' shouted Bee.

'Exactly! Why would you want to go to a stupid party anyway when you can be here?'

And for a moment there was nothing but glee and simple togetherness that sometimes happens when you have a sister like Bee. In that second all worry disappeared and it was nearly impossible to think about the past or the future or anything at all except being where we were.

I wondered if this would do it, if maybe this was the secret gift that had been waiting for us all along. The end of her nightmares and her deluded visions.

The spitty sparks of the fire crackled away. The sky had grown dark, but there were no clouds. We went to the edge of the shore, lay on our backs in the grass, and looked up at the stars.

'We are specks in the universe,' said Bee. 'And now we're going to catch some fish.'

'Bee, look, it's great that we're doing the promise. I'm fine with that, but just don't get your hopes up, OK. Nobody has caught a fish here for years. All the fish are gone. They don't come here any more.'

'That's what you think,' she replied, and she put her small hand on my hand and I could feel the magic in her. At least I thought that was what it was, and I wanted all her dreams to come true.

She plonked herself at the edge, where the sea met the shore and the grass was an unruly row of stringy tufts, where the tide could get so high that you could only see the very tips of the jagged rocks.

'Listen,' she ordered.

We stayed there for ages, the only sound was the sea roaring forward on its way in and sucking backwards on its way out through the tunnels and crevices.

And that was when we heard the strange noise. It was coming from the sea. Bee lifted her head and stared out.

A thing was happening, a thing that nobody would ever be able to explain.

There came a feverish splashing sound and a silvery, shiny light. Her eyes widened and we both stared out over the trembling water.

'My goodness,' said Bee.

The thrashing and splashing in the water got louder and the air seemed to crackle as if fireworks were popping. Except there were no fireworks. There was only Bee and me and the silver light on the water.

'Look,' said Bee, and she pointed slowly at the surface on which a great moving shadow had appeared – wobbling and huge and changing shape the way a storm cloud does.

'Is this magic?' I said.

'No, it's not magic, it's just a message.'

'What is it saying?'

'It's saying, "Look at the secrets that lie beneath the surface! Look at the way the world can surprise you!"'

And Bee's face flashed and shimmered again in the dark.

'It's better than magic. It's a miracle,' said Bee. 'It's mackerel.'

Mackerel usually swim alone or in small groups. But once in a very rare while, they get together in giant shoals, nobody knows why, and in an even rarer while, they get caught in the cove at the edge of Dillon's Park. That was what the silver light was. A giant shoal of mackerel, thrashing around. It grew so noisy we had to shout. Hundreds and hundreds of fish flipping around in the little rocky shoreline.

'This is the best day ever!'

And for ever there will be Bee clear inside my head, standing on the top of Seaweed Rock. And Louie and me dancing and leaping like we were fish ourselves. For a second, she held two live mackerel, in a way you might think was impossible, one in each hand, in the air, and her legs were strong and wet and she was a warrior girl.

Later by the fire, I used the knife the way Uncle Freddy had once shown me, and we cooked the fish. The meat was white and hot and beautiful. The freshest, most delicious, most thrilling food I will ever know.

Our faces were red from the heat of the flames, and our hearts were warm from the togetherness, and by the time we'd finished our bellies were fed and full and a silky quiet had settled around us.

'It's true, isn't it?' Bee's happy voice floated in the air.

'What?' I asked.

'The fish and the shoal and us catching them, and the deliciousness – it's all true. I can put that on the list of real things, can't I?'

'Yes, you can.'

Everything might have turned out differently if Chris Crosby hadn't called me.

'Hello?' I said as if I didn't already know who it was.

'Gracie? Where are you?'

And then I got this idea that it might be great for Chris to come here and see us at our campsite and be part of it all, so I told him. I tried not to take much notice of how his voice had changed, or how it sounded.

'Gracie, yes, I will come. I'll come right now even though it's pretty late, so just for a short while. Is Bee with you?'

'Yeah,'

'OK then, see you there.'

I heard footsteps coming closer and when I zipped open the tent and suddenly I felt sort of naked. No make-up. No decent clothes. Chris was not the only one who had come. Katy was there too. She stared at me all tangled-haired and pale-faced.

'Katy's been very upset about Bee,' he said, a shadow on his face. 'She wanted to make sure Bee was OK.'

'Yeah well, no need. And don't worry. I'm taking care of her, thanks,' I said, climbing out and standing between them and the tent. But there was no avoiding any of this now, and I knew it. Soon Bee was wriggling out too and standing beside me.

'Bee, if you're really so sick, then what are you doing here?' said Katy, her voice stiff and cold.

'I'm not sick. I never was sick. You're the one who was supposed to be sick,' replied Bee.

'I want to know why you didn't come to my party,' said Katy.

'What are you talking about?' said Bee, with her crazy look. 'You had the party without me.'

Chris leaned down and spoke slowly to Bee.

'Your sister pretended you were sick and that you couldn't go to Katy's party. She didn't want you to go. Nobody knows why.'

'But I thought the party was cancelled,' said Bee very quietly.

'Who told you that?' asked Katy.

I could see the realisation reddening Bee's shocked face.

'You, Gracie? You're the reason I didn't get to go?' Bee stared at me. 'Why?'

I couldn't explain it, not to Bee and not to anyone else.

'Go away, everyone. Go away and leave me alone.' She ducked back into the tent and zipped it up from the inside.

A big wind had started to blow. Louie had started to snarl.

I looked at Chris who was frowning back at me.

Little twigs and branches swirled in the air.

'Look, I don't really know what you're up to, but I'm sure you won't be surprised when I tell you that we can't be together any more.'

'You're breaking up with me? Here? In front of Katy?'

'Yes, I am. It's not just about your silly lies and you making my sister and yours so unhappy. I don't care as much about all that. I only came down here because she wouldn't stop pestering me about it. The main thing is, Grace . . . well . . . you're kind of a mess really.'

'A mess?'

'Something about you is falling apart, and to be honest I can't handle anything like that. This is an important year for me. I've a lot on. I can't deal with your . . . your . . . issues.'

'What issues are you talking about?'

'Look, Gracie, I don't want to intrude – it's none of my business really – but I don't think you are the person I thought you were and your family is, well, you're all a bit unstable, I think. I actually don't want to be involved with any of this. I think it's much better if we leave it. I don't think it's going to work out.'

'What do you mean, "work out"? It's not as if I wanted to marry you or anything,' I said, something pounding inside my brain. 'I only wanted to be your girlfriend. I never had any particular long-term plan, just in case that's what you thought.'

'Yeah, well, it's all kind of irrelevant now anyway. It's not going to work.'

He waved his hand up and down in my general direction.

'What do you mean?' I said and I could hear my voice rising and high-pitched even though I was trying to stay calm and keep my dignity.

'I mean, do what you need to do, but don't come near me any more, OK? I am Chris Crosby. And I don't have girlfriends who look like you.'

'What do I look like?'

'You look like a hobo. Plus, just another heads-up, you smell of fish.'

I couldn't think of anything to say after that. I turned slowly, and got back in the tent. I switched on the torch and shone it on myself. I seemed to be speckled with little dots of silver light that were shining out of me. It took me another moment to realise what the dots were.

The mackerel scales had got everywhere – on my jumper and in my hair.

And I looked around this little space not just at me, but at our piled-up sleeping bags, and the curled-up Bee, and Louie stretched out beside her, the three of us smelling of rotting fish and campfire and seaweed and salt.

Somehow it didn't even matter. I was numb. All I wanted to do was tell Bee how sorry I was, but when I tried to speak, it felt as if I was choking, and in the end I wasn't able to. I wanted to explain, but I couldn't.

The wind had started battering the canvas. I had thought it was so sturdy when I'd put it up. Now it felt as flimsy and weak as paper.

'I think we should go home, Bee. I think this was a mistake. I'm sorry I brought you here. Uncle Freddy will start to worry.'

'No,' was all she said then.

Our world had grown twisted and cankered, and there was no room for sorries or explanations, and the silence felt as if it might smother me. I just lay beside her with nothing except guilt and awfulness, not knowing what to say and not knowing what to do.

And that was when Louie began to growl.

People normally don't take Louie's hysteria too seriously. He panics at the sight of a fly and barks when someone turns on the coffee machine. But there was something different about him that day that I still often think about.

It's not just Louie. Watch any dog. If you have a suspicion that your life is about to change for ever, look at your dog first. He'll be the one to tip you off.

I heard a raw kind of noise outside and I peeped out of the tent again. There were birds pecking violently at the flesh of the leftover mackerel and our fire had gone out, leaving a black, charred stain on the grass.

I tried to ask Bee if she was OK, but she turned away from me. She was never going to forgive me, I thought. She was lying on her side, staring at nothing with wide eyes.

I sat beside her. 'Come on, Bee. We can't dwell on this. We have to get up and clean ourselves off and try to be happy.'

No answer.

We must have really stank and so must have our tent but it was obvious that Bee didn't care.

'I wouldn't mind being dead,' was all she said.

The storm was getting worse and, even though she frightened me, I tried to cover it up. I thought I should stay cheerful.

'Hey, Bee, come on. If we died now, these would be our ghost clothes for all eternity. Think about that.'

'I'm not talking about now. I'm talking about someday. Maybe soon. Maybe far away.'

The wind slapped against the tent and somehow the zip opened, splitting the front into its two flaps which started whipping about.

Bee sat up, a sudden streak of terror on her face.

'Oh no,' she whispered. 'Not here, not real. Not outside my head.'

And something shuddered through me too because I knew that she wasn't pretending. I knew she could see something that I couldn't see.

'Help me, Gracie. Gracie, please don't let her in.'

'Who? Don't let who in?'

'The lady. Can't you see her? Look, right there. It's

her. She's real. Look at her, with her no hair and sunken eyes and thin legs – look, over there, standing on the grass. Oh, Gracie, why is she staring at us like that? Oh no.'

'Right, that's it,' I said, 'Bee, this has got to stop now. You're driving yourself mad.'

Bee covered her head with the sleeping bag.

'Gracie, you must stop talking. Be quiet – don't say a word.'

A sound was coming from outside like a wheezy kind of cry.

'Listen to her – listen to her wailing. What in heaven's name is she doing here? What can she want?'

I didn't know what to do. When I shone my torch towards Bee I could see thousands of tiny sweat beads on her little white face. I wrapped my arms around her.

'Oh God, Bee, listen. I think I know what's triggered this. Listen to me. I'm sorry about Katy's party. I thought . . . I thought . . .'

'That's got nothing to do with it! That doesn't matter now. I don't even care,' she said and she clung to me, panting. She was too scared for me to calm her down. Her feelings were too big to fit inside this flimsy tent. It was as though her fear was the storm and the storm was her fear and there was a mad dark moment when I couldn't tell the difference.

I tried. I said, 'Hush,' the way grown-ups do. I stroked

her hair and breathed deeply, hoping that she would too.

'It's only the wind,' I said, and though she repeated it again and again I could tell that she didn't believe it.

'It's only the wind. It's only the wind. It's only the wind.'

And I listened to the outside and I supposed it wouldn't have been that hard to imagine that the wind was a frantic woman out there, keening, howling, screaming from grief and anguish. 'Uncle Freddy, if you're thinking of coming to find us,' I said to myself, 'now would be a good time.' But Uncle Freddy did not come.

It was then that Louie made a dash for it. In less than a second, he was gone from the tent and was off.

'Louie, no!' shouted Bee. And before I could stop her, she ran after him. No one would have ever believed that she could disappear so fast.

SIXTEEN

I grabbed Granddad's torch and I twisted out of the flapping tent.

'They won't be far,' I was talking to myself now, the way mad people do.

The storm had become enormous. Closer up to the sea I could see the waves crashing over Seaweed Rock. If someone had been sitting there now they'd have been knocked off and thrown under.

I sprinted down to the sea and up to the gate and then back to the tent and then all over the park, running in zigzags of dread, calling her name.

And then I heard Louie's bark, distant and strangled by the coiling wind, coming from somewhere up high.

I staggered at a slant against the wind to reach the gap. And I held on to the broken brick and pulled myself through it and got on to the cliff path, even though the gale was raging all around me, and the rickety, wooden steps that I began to climb didn't seem as if they would hold.

I didn't know how I was suddenly certain that this was the direction that Bee had gone in, but the knowledge landed on me.

Sharp rain was falling, spitting into my face. I curled my fist around my torch feeling something very fierce inside me that I had never known.

A single slip, or just one gust of wind, and the rising cliff edge looked as if it might give way. The fall would have been long. Far below, the sea churned and smashed.

I felt the fear that comes with making a desperate and dreadful mistake, and I felt the horror of its terrible result, buried and still unreal, but stirring now, inside my bones. Taking care of her was basically my job. I should have let her go to that stupid party. I was supposed to have quietened the deluded voices inside her – the voices that told her a sunken-eyed woman was out to get her.

I had failed and because of me she had begun this crazy journey to prove something that could never be proved. Believing in something that couldn't be true. Looking for something that wasn't there. Oh, Bee.

I cared about nothing then. Not Uncle Freddy or Chris or Katy's stupid party, or Aunt Lucy. Not Grandfather Patrick; not the memory of my parents. Only Bee.

There was the pain of cold in my hands and confusion as the storm railed all around me and alone in the deafening dark I felt only fear. But it didn't matter. None of it did. For Bee was lost and climbing. Getting to her was the only thing that counted.

Life gets pretty simple when you only have one job. Even if it does make you kind of mental.

Wind can die down in an instant and the world can become deathly quiet again and it can take you a while to notice it.

I slipped on the slime and stone beneath, and the wooden bannister was broken and unreliable under my hand, swaying and creaking as I hung on to it and dragging myself along. My hair stuck to my face, slick and cold as seaweed.

'Bee. Bee,' was the only thing I could say.

The fear did not weaken me. It made me strong, made me angry, made me brave.

Somewhere in the middle of this struggle, everything went still and hushed. And that is when I saw her. At first just a little heap of clothes, but as I battled to get nearer I saw, collapsed in a crumpled pile, that it was Bee. The sight of her made me shiver. All the air came out of me.

'Bee. Bee', I tried to say, but there was no sound. My legs wobbled and my knees hit the muddy ground and I held on to the bottom of one of the wooden posts and fell forward, the ground squelching as my face hit it. When I look back, I still see my knees thudding and all those feelings – of fear and hope – are as real to me still as the rising of the sun.

But then all the things in my head got paler and fainter and Bee's face swam again for a moment in front of me and then blackness. And silence. And nothing.

It wouldn't have come as a surprise to me if we were dead. It wasn't dark any more and birds were singing, and we woke together. 'I found you!' I said to her and she said, 'Thank you for coming,' and I said, 'Come on, they must all be looking for us,' but a tear slid down her muddy face, leaving a wobbly white track. 'Louie,' she said, 'he's gone up there ahead of us. We have to keep going. We have to find him. I know he's up here somewhere and I am not coming down off this cliff until we've got him back. And anyway, look.' Bee pointed.

In the sudden stillness the wild, wobbly path had given way to a mellower, neater place. And my bravery became something else then: astonishment, I thought, and disbelief. Because there were giant candles of different colours – like huge crayons – poking out from the ground, lining a path that looked as if it led somewhere definite. And those coloured candles had coloured flames too, which darted like dancing ghosts.

And in that moment we heard a familiar sound, yet strange too – because of how I felt and where I was. It was Louie's bark, clearer this time, and very close.

'Louie, Louie!' we shouted and, in the silence, his barking kept ringing out.

'What is this?' I whispered to myself. 'Where am I? What's happening?'

Those questions were the fuel that kept each foot following the other. There couldn't be any going back now, Bee knew it and now so did I, not if wild wolves had come out from behind the rocky cliff to drag us away.

'Louie,' we said and our voices sounded like different people – people with nothing to lose any more. And there came a turn in the path and a thickening of the bushes and the line of candles got taller and brighter and it was a miracle they hadn't set the whole side of the bushy cliff on fire. There was a hole in a hedge and the feeling of warmth and nothing to do except climb through, led by the flickering light.

SEVENTEEN

S himmering and gigantic it was, and I was stuck to the ground, staring. It seemed to glisten in front of me like something wet and made of flesh, except it was a building – with a hundred windows and three different turrets and a huge front door that looked to me as if it was wide open.

A great marble statue of a crow came into view and standing beside it was a girl, small and translucent and smiling.

'Welcome,' she said and her voice was a song and her face was white like stone and her hair was streaming with ribbons.

And Bee ran to her and the girl ran to Bee and they jumped up and down like little girls who'd known each other all their lives.

'Who are you?' I asked.

'It's Emily,' Bee said simply.

Emily's voice was low and we had to stand very close to hear.

'You have arrived at exactly the right time, because this . . .' she pointed at the door and the lights inside seemed to glow and twinkle '. . . this is exactly where you need to be right now.'

Something clicked inside my head.

'Emily?' I said. *'Pale* Emily?'

'Yes!' said Bee.

I was silent. I felt dizzy.

'This is Hotel Magnificent,' continued Emily, as if she could hear all the questions banging inside my aching, dazed head. 'And you are very welcome.'

I thought it was the astonishment that made me hear the noise I heard then – a gorgeous, pattering little drumbeat, a most important sound. It was Louie's footsteps racing across a wooden floor, coming towards us, and Bee ran to him.

'Oh, you silly, lovely dog,' she said, 'I thought you were lost, but look – look where he's brought us! Oh, Gracie, see! Look, we are HERE! It's real, Gracie – I'm right. I was right all along. I was right the whole entire time! Isn't it brilliant? It's Hotel Magnificent, and it belongs to the list of real things!'

There was magic in the air and Bee McAuliffe at the centre and I started to see that there were things she understood and things she could picture and things she knew that the world was not able to see.

'Follow me,' she said and suddenly we were inside, and it looked like a concrete, solid place. Not a dream or a story but a proper place that you could walk in and touch and smell and see. And we were there together and excitement and memories and hope and despair bubbled around in this place where all the feelings in the world were possible.

'You came for me, and we came for Louie, and we've made it,' Bee said, laughing and holding my hand and saying how lucky she was to have a sister who was prepared to walk through a storm up a cliff to the vague sounds of the bark of a beloved dog and the uncertain hints of her sister's voice.

Emily floated along beside us, smiling and pointing – first we were in a pale, huge, wooden-floored hallway with golden mirrors all over the walls and two great chairs like thrones.

I was already under a spell, just as she was.

'Isn't there something you need to say to me, Gracie? Me and Louie?' said Bee, scratching the top of Louie's head.

'Like what?'

'Like sorry? Sorry for not believing me. Sorry that you kept telling me Hotel Magnificent wasn't real. Look at it, Gracie. Look at everything!'

She started skipping round the hall, putting her hand on the mirror frames, touching the wax of pillar-sized candles, stroking the marble ledge on the fireplace that was curling with heat from a great log.

172

'Shouldn't we go back down, Bee? They will be looking for us by now. We need to tell everyone that you're safe, that we both are.'

'This is where you are *meant* to be,' repeated Emily, staying near us the whole time, occasionally patting Louie – who'd clearly taken a huge liking to her.

'But we have to get back.'

'Why?' Pale Emily asked.

'Because people will be searching for Bee and Louie and me.'

'Grace McAuliffe,' Pale Emily said, and I wondered vaguely how she knew my full name – how she knew my name at all, 'this is a special place. And now that you're both here, time is frozen – everything is. The world has been stilled for a while and you don't need to be anywhere. Nobody is looking for you. This is one of the things about Hotel Magnificent that you need to understand. There is nowhere else you need to be except here. Besides,' she added, 'it would not do to go struggling down those wooden steps again in these conditions. The storm is not over. We are above it here. It would be quite wrong of you to take your lives into your hands like that,' she beckoned. 'Come this way. There are two hot baths waiting for you with oils and perfume and big dressing gowns.'

'It's the best thing ever!' said Bee and I breathed a sigh of odd relief.

'Come on,' Emily said again. 'This way. And stop worrying.'

I wanted so much for time to stand still, to stop feeling the things I'd been feeling for ages: worried and beaten and lost and cold and small.

Pale Emily pushed open a door with the force of her own hands and the strength of her own body. We followed her down a glittering corridor.

'I've been watching the two of you for the last few months. You two are the reasons I came down. I was sent to rescue you. Bee noticed me straightaway, but you, Gracie, I could have danced in front of you in the middle of maths, in fact I often did, and you'd never have caught the slightest sign of me.'

'You're not making much sense,' I said. 'And anyway, what made you think either of us needed to be rescued?'

'It's OK, Gracie. Honestly, it's OK for us to let her help us.' And at last I looked at Bee, really looked at her, and I tried to imagine what someone else might see if they were looking at her too, and I saw that she was shredded and broken. Her skin was dirty and her clothes were torn and her hair was matted and it would have taken an especially vicious kind of poisonous pride for me not to have accepted this helping hand, no matter how unreal it seemed to be. And then I looked at my arms and they were covered in cuts and scratches too, my fingernails cracked and black, while Pale Emily was all perfect and flowing, her coloured ribbons flying out behind her.

'Come on. Just follow me. Trust someone for once in

your life. You're my big sister and you are the cleverest person I know but sometimes you can be really very silly.'

Music began to play, a harp, I thought, and a violin, and I could hear seagulls squawking, and when I looked up high I could see the windows were wide open. Emily held out her hand and her mottled face seemed to glow.

I thought about how we might start to make our way down again. I thought about what might be waiting for us there. Uncle Freddy all bitter and wrecked, full of despair and dismay and anger. Our campsite, probably putrid and sad.

'I know. I know how hard it is to trust all this,' Pale Emily said. 'I know how unusual it must feel, but give into it. Stop resisting the things you've been trying to put away. It's time to take things out and look at them and touch them with your fingers and see them with your eyes. It's time, Gracie. And I promise you myself, I give you my word, it's going to be fine.'

I followed Pale Emily along the winding, widening corridors of this place with Bee and Louie jostling beside me, and it seemed as if a warm breeze blew into our faces. Pale Emily's feet were so light and she moved so fast that she could have been flying. Maybe she was, and I thought maybe so were we.

Bee was gripped with a mad kind of energy, her eyes fixed on Emily's ribbons. And every time I thought I should just shake myself to wake up from this dream, Pale Emily turned her face to me and said, 'we're nearly there.'

Louie barked a delighted bark but, better than that, Bee's voice had got its cheery lilt back.

'It's true. It's a proper thing. A real thing. Not a rumour or a myth or a legend. Real, Gracie. Imagine that!'

There was a black square in a wall at the end of the long corridor. Pale Emily pressed the stone and a door appeared that gave way to a tunnel lit with blazing sticks. The ground was strong underfoot, though it was getting cold now and our breath came out like smoke. Emily's hair streamed out behind her in wavy shininess and her ribbons seemed luminous in the dark. Her little shoes clacked on the stone, her steps solid and sure, and somehow it made a certainty grow inside me so I could imagine that my face was very like Bee's. It wasn't magic. Just knowledge. It was knowing something was behind the rock. If you didn't think anything was behind it, it looked like a square hole. But when you *knew* there was something there, something great that you could reach, that you could touch, then you realised it was a doorway to an elsewhere place.

'This is all completely ordinary to her,' panted Bee. 'All magic people think there's nothing weird about them. For them it's an everyday thing – they're not even slightly amazed by it,' she explained. Then moments later, 'We're here. It's what I've been hoping for. We're finally here.'

'What is this place?' I kept saying to myself, my hands trembling. The feeling was like nothing I'd ever felt before. I was scared, but excited too – there was hope in my heart, something with a future that made me want to reach out my hand. And right then, out of the dark corner, just as I was thinking that, a hand appeared. It held itself out to me. A wave of fright. And then a flood of remembering. I knew it as soon as I saw it – beautiful and old and as familiar as my own.

'I've been expecting you,' said a voice and then he stepped out into the light.

Granddad. All of him. Whole and breathing and warm and alive-looking.

He wrapped his old arms around us as we wrapped ours around him like we always used to.

Bee's lovely sobbing was like no other, an intricate sound full of waves of grief and love, and threads of longing and loss, and splodges of memory. And millions of tiny bubbles of relief.

'Oh, my wounded heart,' was all she could say.

'My dears, there were so many other things I had still wanted to do. I hadn't been in the slightest bit ready to go, but you see, events overtook me, and in the end it wasn't my choice. I suppose it rarely is.'

He hadn't taken to death very well. 'I must confess, I'm

having rather a difficult time adjusting. It's the reason I'm here.'

'What is it though – what is this place?' I asked again, this time out loud.

'Oh, it's perfectly nice, comfortable inside, and I must say the people are terrific. But you see the problem is that Hotel Magnificent is neither here nor there. Not one thing or another.

'There were so many things that I still needed to take care of. I feel responsible for what has happened to you since I left. Emily has been a godsend of course, and needless to say I've always been able to send urgent messages through Louie, which has been a blessing. But you know Louie, he's not the most reliable conveyer of information. His heart's in the right place but he so often picks up the wrong end of the stick.'

Louie wagged his tail, happily oblivious.

We told Granddad everything. About Aunt Lucy and Chris Crosby and the ski trip and the party and the tent and the mackerel and the storm. But I got this feeling that he already knew. About everything.

'Rest and recuperation for the lost and the desperate,' Granddad said that was the mission of Hotel Magnificent and I thought what a nice thing it was for a building to have a mission, especially one as lovely as that.

'I'm afraid it's only temporary, but for the moment, this is your refuge and warmth. It is your retreat as it is mine.

We both have places to go after here, but right now you get to stay still for a little while and to declare what it is you need.'

'We need everything,' said Bee. 'There is an ocean of sadness inside us.'

And Bee was crying again and Grandfather was telling her that sadness was all right and that he felt sad too and how brilliant it was to see us and how just looking at our faces made him happier than he could explain.

I don't know how long we cried for, but nobody told us to stop. You might have thought that crying would be sad, which of course it was, but in the end it turned out to be sort of funny. At least we stopped crying from sadness and began laughing from something else: amazement, strangeness, surprise.

Pale Emily took us to a pink-lit place and it's hazy now and I can't really remember how but somehow our filthy clothes were gone and we wore dresses all floaty, with flowers in our hair, and we smelled of lemons and of rose petals.

'Just like a fairy tale, only real!' said Bee.

'Look at us,' she said, when we returned to Granddad.

'You are beautiful,' Granddad said, 'but,' he held up a wise finger. 'you are always beautiful, whether clean or dirty, fragrant or not. Now come this way.'

And we followed him then through muffled hallways, past lighted fireplaces, between golden pillars and under glittering candelabras.

Eventually, Granddad Patrick stopped at a door and pushed it open.

That room.

Every day, for the rest of my life, it will flash inside my head and it will fill me with light.

EIGHTEEN

In the middle was a long table laid with golden knives and forks and silver-rimmed plates and big glass goblets and great water jugs stuffed with lemon wedges and green herbs. And I could smell something else unmistakeable: roasted almonds. Melted marshmallows.

We walked in. There were already lots of people around the table and there was the clinking of glasses and little bursts of genuine, friendly laughter. I felt all their eyes turn towards us and then those same eyes turned back towards two people sitting at the very end. Granddad Patrick walked right up to sit on one side of them and there were two empty places on the other.

'Is that where we're supposed to sit?' I asked Bee, who for the first time since we'd arrived didn't seem to know anything at all. The closer we got, the tighter Bee's hand gripped mine. And then, as we got closer still, she began to whimper.

'Oh no,' she said, 'I've got to go.'

'Em, Bee, what are you doing?' I said quietly behind clenched teeth. 'Come on. You're the reason we're here. And I think this dinner is for us. I'm not doing this on my own. I'm not letting you blow it up.'

'Yes, but, look,' she said, pulling away from me and beginning to do her backwards walk. 'I think I actually am going to have to sit this one out after all. You have a lovely time. I'll just head back now, I know the way. Emily says I can go to her room if I want, and in any case I'm not that hungry, and anyway Emily says she will bring cherries and pineapple whenever I want. I'll be fine.'

Bee's eyes were very wide and round and she was breathing fast with a sheen of sweat on her face.

'What? What is it, Bee?'

She was pointing to the woman we were supposed to sit beside and, as my eyes adjusted, I saw her too. No hair. Sunken eyes. Even greyer and paler than anyone else in the room. Thin, but smiling at us.

'She's the one – she's the one who's been haunting me. She's the scary lady in my nightmares, and who came to me in the tent. I can't possibly sit beside her. It's her. She's the one who's been frightening me all this time. Gracie, please don't make me go near her. Let me go.'

Bee lifted up her dress and turned around and began to run towards the door.

'I'll go after her,' said Granddad. 'This might take her a

while.' And all the guests nodded their heads and by then I was close enough to see that the two people at the top of the table were looking at me very strangely, their eyes full of tears.

Something inside me pinged as though I were an instrument that some gifted person had begun to play.

'Mum?' I said. 'Dad?'

And they were nodding their heads and holding their arms out to me and the rest of the table began to clap and cheer. It was them and I was remembering things that I didn't realise I even knew, and their arms were like an old, old place that I'd been aching for my whole life. And the mist cleared.

I'd been searching for sense. I'd been trying to make meaning out of this, the strangest of places. I hadn't understood what it was doing here and since I'd arrived I'd been asking why. And all this time it was them. They were the reason.

And right then I remembered her. Not the beautiful mother of the photographs and my old memories but other things that I had forgotten: her sickness and her paleness and her weakness, and the dark smudges under her eyes and all her beautiful hair gone.

It wasn't that no one had tried to talk to me about what had happened. Uncle Freddy had tried lots of times, I remembered that now too, and how I'd put my hands up to my ears and how I had begun to shout.

'La-la-la-la,' I'd said. And I remembered how I had hammered my nine-year-old fists on his chest and he hadn't got cross with me at all.

Doctors could cure a lot of people who got sick, but they hadn't been able to fix my mum.

'Hello, my darling,' she said at first.

And my dad said, 'Gracie, we can't tell you how much we've been dying to see you,' and everyone around the table laughed – the kind, generous laugh that people do when someone is trying to lighten the mood of a highly emotional moment.

They said we'd be able to talk lots more, but for now it was enough for us to be in the same space, for me to hear their voices, strange and familiar, and for them to look at me and look at me and look at me. They didn't eat a single thing and neither did I but somehow it helped to be surrounded by others who smiled and nodded and wished us well.

Bee could be with Granddad while I was to spend time with my parents and it was kind of a relief not to have to be thinking about her for a little while, so they could tell me everything.

They told me the whole story, the one I needed to hear.

'Exactly two days after I died, your dad died too,' said Mum.

'Of a heart attack,' added Dad, helpfully.

It had been so unspeakable and so unhearable to me for so long.

'I hadn't wanted to leave you. I didn't go on purpose, it's just that sometimes grief can turn your body into a walking catastrophe.'

Before he'd dropped dead, blinded and beaten by sadness, he'd smashed all the downstairs windows in our house with his fist. Mum interjected to say she'd no idea what go into him. Totally out of character.

'I've always felt terrible about it,' he said.

'It's OK, Dad. People do crazy things when their hearts are broken.'

And speaking of broken hearts, I got the chance to tell them about Chris Crosby, and how great it had been at first, and how because of Aunt Lucy I'd been able to go on the ski trip and everything had been more or less perfect, me as happy as I'd ever imagined I'd be, and how I'd been a member of the top group and how hardly anyone got to be that.

They nodded and listened and looked at each other the way I imagined parents would when their daughter was telling them about stuff that was going on in her life.

I told them about how horrible Chris had suddenly become and how he'd broken up with me partly because of the thing about Katy's party but mostly because I didn't look good enough for him – that he saw me all messy with no make-up and he decided he didn't like me any more. And I told them that Aunt Lucy had come back into everyone's life and not everyone was too happy about it, especially not Uncle Freddy who was angry with her – very angry.

They knew about the tent and the mackerel and about Aunt Lucy coming back. I didn't even feel amazed.

Aunt Lucy had come back to our house because my mum had asked her to promise that wherever she was in the world, she would come home and help take care of us.

They explained something I already sort of knew: Aunt Lucy wasn't selfish or manipulative or controlling or judgemental. She was full of love. She wanted to do what she had promised to do. She wanted us to be happy. She'd gone to a lot of trouble to keep her promise.

Uncle Freddy was wrong about her, and so was Bee. I knew the whole story. I didn't need my parents to tell me that Aunt Lucy's motives were good and pure. I'd always known. I'd known the very moment she arrived. She was my kindred spirit. She was my link to my parents. She wanted things for me that nobody else had even known I needed.

'You mustn't be too hard on your uncle either,' said my dad, but I couldn't stop thinking about Bee and Uncle Freddy and how stubborn they could be and how they'd never really given Aunt Lucy a chance.

My parents had come down to see us loads of times. I thought about the shadows at the side of my vision that I'd sometimes seen, and I realised it had been them. They'd really been haunting me. It hadn't been just some flash of memory, some yearning of my imagination. It had been them, hanging around, trying to do their best to guard over us, even though they were dead.

Bee couldn't stay hiding wherever she was with Granddad, but she was scared of Mum – the lady with no hair and sunken eyes. What Bee had seen as someone coming with bony hands to snatch her was really my mum reaching for her with aching love.

'Bee thought you were some demon trying to kill her,' I said before I realised how tactless it could have sounded.

But Mum didn't seem too insulted. She said she understood. 'I don't know how I'll ever leave properly if I can't spend some time with her too.'

Dad said he thought it was going to be OK. 'Look,' he said to Mum, pointing towards the mirror.

Mum stood to look at herself, and that was when I noticed what was happening too. Her sunken sickness was changing. Slowly, she was becoming beautiful again. And the more I noticed, and looked, the more she seemed to change. I watched as her hair began to grow and her skin regained a kind of goldenness that is impossible to describe.

And don't ask me to explain any of this because I cannot.

But she came back. Back to the mother of our photographs with her wavy hair and her watchful eyes and her crooked smile.

'Oh, Mum, you were so sick,' I said.

'I was, darling. And you were very young.'

'Yes, but look,' said Dad, 'look – she is well again. We both are. See us!'

Mum and Dad gave me satin slippers and we floated down to a huge ballroom which had shiny floors and great lights and there was music and lovely singing in the background. The three of us danced together and laughed and held hands and they came back to me and there was nothing but the smell of melted marshmallows and roasted almonds. It was safe and warm and happy and part of me wanted never to go back down, to stay dancing in a circle like that for ever.

I didn't really want Bee interfering with all of this but the door opened then and Granddad and Bee were there. We stopped dancing and Bee was a tiny figure in the huge doorway with Louie shaking beside her. She sighed and breathed out a word as if she'd been holding it in for a long, long time:

'Mama,' she said, as if she were small again.

I had to stand aside. It wouldn't have been right not to. And Bee did her crazy limb-flinging run all the way over to them, elbows and feet and arms all over the place, tears dripping off the end of her chin. My dad picked her up and swung her around and then my mum stood right in the middle of this echoey ballroom and it didn't matter how strange it was because Bee was clinging to our mum and our mum was clinging to her.

'Oh, my darling love.' Mum's whisper echoed around the room like a secret song. 'I never meant to frighten you. It was the last thing I would have wanted to do. I can't bear that I scared you and left you and abandoned you, and your sister.'

'We're sorry, sweetheart,' said Dad. 'We're so very sorry.'

And all Bee kept saying was, 'It's OK, Mama. It's OK, Dada. It's OK.'

And for the first time it did feel OK, in that beautiful room with music playing. Everyone was together, including Louie, who rushed around us all like a hairy force field. And I never will forget.

There were lots of things we said to each other and at the centre of it was all of us doing what we could to make sense of the things that didn't make sense at all.

Pale Emily popped in a lot.

'How is everybody getting on?' she would ask and Mum and Dad would say, 'Perfectly,' together at exactly the same time and she would say, 'Oh, jolly good – I am glad. You can never be sure.'

And somehow Pale Emily seemed less pale and it no longer seemed as if I could see through her.

'She's starting to remind me of somebody,' said Bee dreamily, and I knew what she meant but neither of us could quite put our finger on who, and anyway, time with our parents was precious and it felt as if there was still so much to say.

'Oh goodness, but Bee had only been such a tiny little one when we . . . when we . . .' Dad said.

'Having to leave you, that was the worst thing about it,' continued Mum. 'And you see we've been missing you both so deeply and dreadfully all this time. It felt impossible and wrong for us to disappear from your lives . . . which is why we were never able to, not completely.'

'It's not really the done thing,' Dad said, 'but we found we couldn't stop ourselves. We've been coming back all this time.'

They explained how they had got into the habit of visiting us. It was never for any big event or anything. Just the small things such as watching us as we slept and seeing us safely to school and making sure we didn't drown down by the shore or fall off my bike.

Bee had always known someone was there and from time to time, so had I.

'It's pretty great to learn that I wasn't going mad – that it was the two of you.' They both looked delighted when I said that.

Mum got to tell us quite a few things:

'Your Uncle Freddy and your Aunt Lucy and I used to camp in Dillon's Park when we were young. We wanted you to have the same experience, feel the same magic.

Granddad was sure it would be fine. We're sorry it turned out the way it did.'

'It turned out great. It brought us to you.'

'Ah, yes, indeed, of course, so it did.'

'And by the way, Gracie,' Dad said as he held me by the shoulders in kind of the same way Bee always did, 'as far as we are concerned, you are worth a hundred Chris Crosbys. If he doesn't want to be with you then it's his loss. You're more beautiful and lovely and clever than he could ever be.'

'Agreed,' chimed in Granddad Patrick who kept appearing in the room without us noticing. 'Even when you're smelling of mackerel.'

Everybody laughed and it was a most lovely sound.

I didn't know exactly how long we were in Hotel Magnificent for. It felt like ages and it felt like no time at all. I guess it is just as Pale Emily explained: you get to stay in a place for as long as you need, which in our case was long enough for my parents to become ordinary to us again.

In the end, they were like a building you hadn't been in since you were a kid. Smaller than I remembered. They were still lovely, but slowly, Bee and I stopped being quite so enchanted or dazzled by them. Which was good, I thought.

'It's not the job of grown-ups to dazzle you,' Granddad told me. 'The real job of grown-ups is to get you ready to

be dazzled by everything else.'

NINETEEN

We couldn't stay there for ever. I guess I'd known that from the start. I didn't think anyone would have wanted us to, not even Mum and Dad.

'Why do people not believe in a place like this?' Bee asked Pale Emily.

'Many reasons,' she replied. 'A lot of people don't pay attention to the details that prove we are here. Many dwell so much in the rational, explainable world that they cannot see it is only a tiny fraction of everything, and they don't use their courage or creativity to look for the very things, the very people, who might provide them with refuge and strength. It's a bit annoying not to be believed in.'

'Gosh, I'm so sorry – I had no idea,' I said.

'I always believed,' boasted Bee. 'And I am very glad because I don't think our broken hearts would have mended if we hadn't come.'

'Ah well, you see now, broken-heartedness is a much

over-diagnosed condition, and it is actually very rare. Many people feel as if their hearts are broken but it's usually not the case. Your hearts have been hurting, for sure, your hearts have been aching, no doubt, but it takes a special kind of disaster to break hearts and I am glad to say that despite the terrible difficulties you have faced in your short lives, both yours are entirely intact.'

That very second, in the gap of our silence, I remembered the sound of our Uncle Freddy's voice.

What happened next happened very quickly. First, Louie's bark rose to a frenzy. And then Emily came running up the big swirling staircase. At first I couldn't make it out, but as she got closer I could hear her saying one word over and over again: 'TIME, TIME, TIME.' The ground beneath us began to shudder and bits of stone and marble fell from the ceiling. The great wooden floors started to crack and the whole of Hotel Magnificent shook and began to crumble.

And then Grandfather's voice became wild and huge.

'IF YOU DON'T ALL GET OUT NOW YOU'RE GOING TO BE STUCK HERE FOR EVER. THE GIRLS, THEY HAVE TO LEAVE. YOU MUST GET OUT! GET OUT OF HERE!'

Louie ranged about, trying to round up me and Bee, as if it was his job.

And it was my mum then who looked small and lost and it felt as if I was the grown-up, and as if whatever I said just then was going to matter very much for a long time – maybe for ever. And this was what I did say.

'I will think about how it felt to be so close to you that I could hear the beating of your heart. I will remember your singing, and I will remember the way you laughed. I remember the porridge you used to make with the blueberries in it and I remember us splashing around in the mud. Mum, I remember your hair, long and wavy and silky, and I will remember what it was like to put my fingers through it. It doesn't really matter how much time goes by. I'll bring it all with me. You'll always be with us.'

When I look back, I know it was only a glimpse. It wasn't everything they were, and all the things they did and all the love they had. It was only a tiny slice. And that was all I got, but it doesn't matter. They are in me.

Bee had seemed so wise and so ready but now I could see she had changed her mind.

'It's the end,' she said with a mystical look in her eye, and she swept over to throw her arms around Mum and hold on very tight.

'I need them, Gracie. I've been trying to live without them but I don't think I can do it any more.'

Oh, Bee.

'Children, everything is sliding and none of us will be able to stay.'

Bee was holding on to Mum, her little hands clasped to her arms, and she was saying, 'I'm staying with you, Mum, wherever you're going, I don't care – I don't mind if we slide into the ocean together or float up into the sky. I'm not going to let you leave me.'

I could see Granddad standing at the entrance. He was our only hope.

'Granddad. Talk to her! Please, we have to go back. Bee doesn't understand. If she stays then she will be . . . She will be. . . She will be . . .'

I couldn't say it. I could not use the word I'd been so afraid of for so long. Dead. Dead. Deadness. The thing that had ruined our lives.

It was never going to be an easy goodbye, but Granddad soothed Bee.

'Bee, there are many people down there who care about you and you must be with them. It wouldn't be right. And anyway, you have Grace, who's always going to take care of you – aren't you, Grace, my darling?'

'I will. I will take care of Bee, always,' I promised them all.

I'm not exactly sure what it was that made her change her mind, but in the middle of this love and this rush and this panic, I could see something turning around in Bee, because she said: 'And I will take care of Grace.' And it was a promise and I knew she was going to do everything to keep it.

Louie was snarling now in his quest to bring us back to our lives, tugging at my lovely dress and ripping the bottom of it, and we had to let them go.

'You are great and we love you. We always will,' they said, and we told them we loved them too.

'Girls, you are our gift,' said Dad.

I think it was that – being called their gift – which was the thing that gave us courage. We waved and we smiled and Louie went first, and then doubled around to make sure we were coming. Together, the three of us made our way down the narrow cliff path.

'Don't turn around. Hold on tight to the rail. Don't look back,' they shouted.

And we both knew and felt and kept the strange, sad joy that came from the brief, clear glimpse of things we had lost.

I held Bee's hand all the way to the muddy patch where we had fallen on the way up and Bee stopped there and sat on the ground. I sat too and Louie stood over us, looking up and then down, and the wind had got big and crazy again and we held on to each other, not able to go any further. Stuck there on the edge of the cliff. I was dizzy and everything went blank. I closed my eyes.

When we woke, everything had changed back again.

Hotel Magnificent was gone. Only huge boulders of twinkling granite were left, wedged into the cliff.

TWENTY

'Thank goodness,' said Uncle Freddy, his voice hoarse. Our dresses were gone too. We were back in our old clothes, smelling horrible. Fishier than ever. I couldn't figure it out. I probably never will.

'Darling Uncle Freddy, you've climbed these heights for us!' sighed Bee.

Aunt Lucy was close behind. He pulled us towards him, and turned around to call to her.

'It's all right, Lucy, I have them.'

He'd brought Granddad's silver-tipped walking stick. I handed it to Bee. Together we were able to make our way down.

And at the bottom of the hill in Dillon's Park there was a small crowd of people. Janine and Lal and Gertie and the Misses Allen and even two of my teachers, and Scully. They circled around us and none of them seemed to mind how filthy we were. All of them jumped around and cheered and even though my heart was heavy I still felt strong and the ground underneath my feet felt solid.

The storm had calmed and the air felt lighter as it often does when morning comes, and everyone came back to our house for tea. After they'd gone, Uncle Freddy and Aunt Lucy stayed in the kitchen for ages, and we listened from our room upstairs.

'If they hadn't been safe, if something had happened to them, I would have never forgiven myself,' said Uncle Freddy.

'You really do love them, don't you?' said Aunt Lucy.

'Of course I do,' Uncle Freddy said. 'What did you think? I've missed you, Loosey Goosey, I've hated you being away for so long.'

We were amazed to hear him call her something like that.

'I've missed you too, Fredser,' she said.

And we heard her say a whole load of other things as well. About not being able to face her sister's death. About how she'd felt so helpless and hopeless. About how sorry she was for leaving us all. About thinking that if she went away and tried to make a success of something then maybe she could come back and keep her promises. And she had. She'd worked all over the world, she said, with a fierceness of someone who wanted to forget about everything else.

And their voices sounded younger, and it seemed

almost as if, for a second, the two of them were little kids themselves.

A few days later Uncle Freddy and Aunt Lucy decided to throw a party. We framed photos of our parents that we'd chosen from the biscuit tin, and left them in places where everyone could see. Aunt Lucy had brought a photo of her own of my mum and Uncle Freddy and Aunt Lucy when they were kids. They were sitting in front of a tent and it was definitely Dillon's Park because you could see the grass and the spongy ground and in the corner of the picture, the foam and glitter of the sea.

When a party is perfect, nobody wants a single person to leave, and nobody wants a single person to arrive, and that was how it felt. The music and the food and the bursts of laughing and the clusters of people. And Bee floating around in her pale yellow dress, happy and perfect herself, and Aunt Lucy with diamonds in her hair. She smiled at me and for a brief moment I thought she was my mum, come down one last time to say goodbye. Aunt Lucy and my mum have the same smile and the same earlobes, just different hair.

Of course if I thought about it, there were people missing, but we were not so strangled from the loss of them and something lightened inside me. The dead stay in your heart if you let them. And I did – I remembered them fully, all the sadness and all the happiness and everything.

Nobody noticed the shadow at the front door at first and then, when we did, it was Uncle Freddy who said he would open it. It was someone for me, he said.

Chris Crosby.

I went to the door and waited to see how I was going to feel or what was going to happen.

'Gracie, I've changed my mind. I don't want to break up with you,' he said, smiling. 'I feel terrible for all you've been through. I know how gutted you must have been when I told you we were breaking up and I understand – and it's probably why you disappeared with your sister and everyone was worried. But let's put it behind us. OK? I mean, you look so good again, and you seem fine, and I am here.'

I waited for his talking to stop and I held on to the frame of our front door to steady myself.

'Chris, I think you should go home.'

'What?' His smile faded a little.

'I'm going to meet a lot of people in my life, and I'm going to kiss a few of them, and some of them I'll fall in love with. But from now on the ones I'm going to love are going to love me back, not just when I have make-up on my face, not just when I'm strong and happy but all the other times too, including when I'm broken and on my knees and I smell bad.'

'But I'm Chris Crosby,' he said, looking mystified. 'And I've told you I want you back.'

'Yes and I am Grace McAuliffe, and being with you is not the measure of me. The measure of me is how loudly I sing when all feels as if it is lost. How I've been able to get out of bed even when my heart was dark with sadness.'

'I actually don't know what you mean,' he said and I told him it was OK. He didn't have to know because, amazingly enough, it actually wasn't about him.

'But I want you back,' he repeated.

'Yeah well, you're not getting me.'

It was definitely the first time in his life anyone had said that to Chris Crosby.

He had grown pale, and I felt a little bit sorry for him, but mostly I felt strong, and certain, and calm, and I felt I knew myself and I was letting something go. I felt the start of something new. I watched him as he walked away.

The party was buzzing and I decided that it would be fine without me, for a little while, and Louie looked as if he could do with a walk on the beach too.

I hadn't been down there for very long when I heard a noise and it was Bee scrambling along the rocks, a fishing rod in her hand.

'Gracie. Goodness! I can't tell you how glad I am to find you! Let's see if we can catch some fish.'

*

It turned out that everyone in her class loved Bee greatly. I had been the only one who'd thought she was weird. Everyone else thought she was lovely and funny and sweet and clever and loyal and friendly. I should have been proud of her all that time, but I was weighed down with things that had been poisoning me. She and Katy became even better friends and I was relieved when everyone seemed to forget about the misunderstanding with the party and thankful about how little it mattered in the end.

Bee had loads to fill the Misses Allen in on, though she was a bit disappointed to find out that there was very little they didn't know already. They knew the exact location of Hotel Magnificent. They'd learned about it, they told her, from their sister Emily who'd sadly drowned a long time ago when the three of them were children, before they'd learned to swim.

Scully was delighted that I wasn't part of Chris's group any more. 'Do you ever miss being up there at the top table?' he asked one day when we were eating sandwiches in the yard with everyone else.

'Nah,' I said. 'It wasn't nearly as much fun as everyone thinks. Sometimes it was actually kind of boring.'

'What do they talk about?'

'The same things that everyone talks about, I guess, just in louder voices.'

Scully said that real friendships stand the test of time. And he's right.

In memory of Granddad, we kept the poker parties going. We shouldn't have been at all surprised that the Misses Allen knew how to play. 'Demons at it,' they revealed one day in the library, which was when we said they should come too. Lal and Gertie were delighted to keep up the tradition. Scully taught Aunt Lucy and Janine the rules – and before long Aunt Lucy, a wizard with numbers, became so frighteningly good at figuring out the odds that we ended up persuading her not to play, after all.

A few times Scully asked me about what had happened that night we were lost, but I never could explain.

He told me how scared everyone had been and how cold and strange Dillon's Park had felt when the search party assembled – the Misses Allen, Janine, Scully, Uncle Freddy, Aunt Lucy – that small but fierce and loyal army of people who love us and care about us, and will always want us to be OK.

When I am older and when my sister Bee is too, maybe we will have children of our own. And I hope we'll teach them how to sleep under tents in Dillon's Park and to fish on Seaweed Rock. And I am sure I will long to protect them from sadness too, just as Uncle Freddy wanted to do for us. But I will know I cannot do that. They will have to hold on to life with all of its sorrows and confusions and sadnesses and joys because that's basically what life is full of – as surely as the grass in Dillon's Park grows out of the spongy ground, as surely as the fish swim sparkling and deep under the water, as surely as the sun glints and flashes on the old granite boulders where Hotel Magnificent used to be.

The Misses Allen say that Hotel Magnificent hasn't really gone away. According to them, the boulders high up at the back of Dillon's Park are still doorways, and they wait for people who are lost, because they know they will come, and when they do, that magic place will reappear, its candles twinkling and its doors open. The smell of perfume and protection and courage will draw the lost ones in and they will be rescued by a fairy-tale building that most people think doesn't even exist.

Bee says we have proof now because we were there and we saw it ourselves. Personally, I don't really know any more. As time goes by, I've grown less certain about what actually happened up there that night. But still, now, there are things I will always be sure of: that even the smudgiest memories can become rich and pure; that you can see again the faces of the ones you have loved; that if you hold on tight, you will not fall; that if you're lucky, you have a list you can depend on – a list of real things. And sometimes the list is longer than you think.

ACKNOWLEDGEMENTS

I thank my children, Eoghan, Stef and Gabbie, to whom this book is dedicated, who tolerate and support their mother's random disappearances and who don't get mad when the pasta boils over.

As ever, thank you Jo Unwin, literary agent and cherished friend. Thank you, Helen Thomas for the tender-eyed insight that makes you so brilliant. Thanks to that irreplaceable two-person team of trusted first readers: Ben Moore and Melanie Sheridan whose creativity and honesty have nourished me in so many ways, not just while this book was being written. A special word of thanks to Fiona Kennedy from whose talent and wisdom I have learned so much.

By some extraordinary stroke of undeserved luck, while writing this book, I have been blessed by guidance and inspiration from other writers, including lifelong friends Eoin Devereux and Joseph O'Connor, and newly found mentors: Louise O'Neill, Donal Ryan, Mary O'Malley, Julian Gough, Bob Burke, Dan Mooney, Iva Yates and Noel Harrington. It has also been a huge privilege to witness the writing journeys of the MA students of creative writing at the University of Limerick. I'm fairly convinced that their collective belief in the power of story is enough to create a whole new source of alternative energy that could sustain the world.

Thanks once more and forever to Elizabeth Moore and to Paul, Meredith, David, Morgan and Alma Rose. Thanks also to Anne, John, Susan, John, Annmarie, Gearoid, Hugh, Ashlee, Sophie, Abby, Moya and Zoe.

Finally, thanks to Ger Fitz. You're a gorgeous man and I love you.

SARAH MOORE FITZGERALD grew up in Dublin and lives near Limerick where her work as an academic focuses on researching the ways in which people learn best. Since becoming a published novelist, she also teaches creative writing at the University of Limerick and at the Frank McCourt Summer School in New York City. She is a founding member of 'WritePace' a Limerick-based writers' group which meets monthly in the City Library. She lives in County Clare with her husband Gerard Fitzgerald and their three children.

Read the first chapter of

THE APPLE TART OF HOPE

THE FIRST SLICE

They had to have an ambulance outside the church in case someone fainted. Men with green armbands directed the traffic. Someone had written 'FULL' in red on a sign and hung it on the entrance to the car park. Neighbours opened their gates.

Inside, big strips of paper had been taped to the backs of the first four rows of seats on which another sign said, 'Reserved for 3R' because only the people in his class were allowed to sit there.

Everyone looked dazed. It was the Day of Prayer for Oscar Dunleavy, who was missing, presumed dead – and no one ever gets used to something like that.

Father Frank was at the absolute centre of everything. He said that Oscar's classmates were going to need space and protection and respect on account of the 'unnatural, wretched, disbelieving things' you feel when a person in your class looks like they are never going to be seen again.

We were also going to need blankets because the heating in the church had broken down just when the February weather had taken another turn for the worse.

I heard Father Frank talking to the parents about how we were 'in for a very difficult time' – facing Oscar's empty desk, and passing his still-padlocked, graffitied locker that nobody had had the heart to wrench open. Father Frank was in his element, focusing on something more important than his usual duties, which normally involved going round the school telling people to pick up their rubbish or to spit out their chewing gum.

Now he was soothing people who were sad and traumatised, and talking a language of grief and comfort that it turns out he is fluent in.

He explained that even when it looked as if everyone was fine, we were going to encounter bewildering moments when the loss of Oscar would be like an assault on our impressionable young minds, not only during these empty sad weeks, but for many years to come.

Everybody filed in. Pale faces. Blotchy red noses. The whole class melded into one single silent smudge, a blue blur of uniforms shimmering like a giant ghost.

Every time I looked at the crowd, I saw something I didn't want to see: a grown man's face quivering, a woman rustling in her bag for a tissue, tears dropping off the end of someone's chin. There were low murmured hellos and unnatural-sounding coughs.

And then there was Oscar's dad, pushing Stevie's wheelchair, the two of them looking like the broken links of a chain. For a second, the squeal of someone's baby drifted above us – an accidental happy little noise ringing out, clear and pure in the middle of the despair. There were flowers, tons and tons of flowers, all blue and yellow.

'Cornflower. Buttercup,' said Father Frank somewhere in the middle of his endless speech.

'Cornflower for the blue of his blue eyes. Buttercup for his bright soul.' Seriously, that's actually what he said.

There was something in the air that smelled of herbs and musk. Dust seemed to rise from corners of the church like an unearthly kind of mist. And for the duration of this unwanted ceremony, everyone in my class seemed to be trying their best not to look into each other's eyes.

I was on the verge of assuming that Father Frank's speech really was going to go on for ever, but then his voice got deeper and slower and more solemn, signalling the end of something and the beginning of something else.

'Ahem,' he said, 'now we're going to ask Oscar's best friend to come forward, please, for her reading. She was the person closest to Oscar. She is going to say a few words in memory of her friend – on behalf of all of us who knew him and loved him so well.'

I could feel myself heating up with that embarrassment

you get when you're not prepared for something important. Nobody had said anything to me about a reading. I wasn't in the mood to stand up in front of anyone or say anything. But I took a couple of deep breaths and I told myself that I had to keep it together for Oscar. I felt sure that the words I was supposed to read would be up there on the stand beside Father Frank, waiting for me. Someone was meant to have cleared this with me in advance, and there must have been a mix-up because nobody had, but I guessed that was probably understandable under the distressing circumstances.

Nobody was hovering nearby, waiting to give me instructions and all I could see was the tops of everyone's heads. I got to my feet as the silence bulged inside the church and people shifted around on the benches. The crowd seemed to quiver in front of me.

And then she stood up. Golden-haired and glittery, rising like an angel from her seat and walking so gracefully to the top of the church that it looked as if she was floating. At the sight of her, I was thick-footed – stuck to the floor. The angel girl proceeded to the microphone.

'Who is that?' I asked my mum, who did not know.

'Who,' I leaned over to Andy Fewer who was sitting in the row in front of me, 'is that?' And as the girl began to speak I realised that I'd seen the outline of her before and I did know who she was.

'*Death is nothing at all . . .*'

Her voice was like melted chocolate and it drifted among

us, as if music had begun to play.

'. . . *one brief moment and everything will be as it was before.*'

Andy turned to me with a mystified look.

'That's Paloma,' he said as if I'd asked him what planet we were on. 'Paloma Killealy.'

'Of course,' I thought. 'Of course it's her.'

When she'd finished the reading, she said there was this song that was Oscar's favourite, like, ever, and how whenever she heard it, she'd always think of him.

'This is for you, Osc,' she said, and she started to sing some song that I did not recognise.

Osc? Since when was that his name? Nobody ever called him that.

When something bad happens to someone young, and when people get together in a church to say prayers for that person, there is a weird vibration, sort of like a buzz or a whistle. Everything shudders, like I reckon it would at the beginning of an earthquake, as if even the ground is shocked and horrified by the wrongness of it all.

'*There should have been so much time ahead of him,*' was the kind of obvious, useless thing that everyone kept repeating, not that anything anyone said was going to make a single bit of difference – at least not now. It was too late, they said. Because Oscar had made his decision, and we were going to have to suffer for the rest of our lives because of it. He was

gone. And by now, everyone more or less took it for granted
that he wasn't coming back.

February had been Oscar's favourite time of the year.

I'd told him he must be the only person in the universe
with a pet month, but he was quite stubborn about it.
He explained that when you stop being a kid, Christmas is
nothing but a terrible disappointment. And January has never
been anything but a dark and boring month full of homework
and dull dinners. But then, right at that moment when the
world seems to be at its bleakest, February creeps up on you
like a best friend you haven't seen in a while, tapping you on
the shoulder.

Plus, this particular February had been holding up a new
sign, allowing us to make plans to do things that none of us
had ever done before – exciting stuff – different stuff – teenage
stuff. We weren't little kids any more and this February had
been full of a hundred different kinds of new chances.

Now, any of the chances Oscar might ever have had, had
dropped radically. To nil.

Outside, on the steps of the church it was formal and hushed,
but there was a low murmur that felt as if it was growing,
like some distant, gigantic monster was moving closer by the
second.

A group of parents clustered round Father Frank, and the sun shone like a cruel joke, making everything seem more beautiful than it deserved to be. Andy was there, and so was Greg, and Father Frank was asking, 'Deary deary me, boys, why? Why would someone with so much going for him have . . . have . . . ended it all in the way he appears to have done?'

'Oh Father, you see, it could be for any number of reasons,' Andy said, serious and fluent, as if he was an expert on the subject. 'Personally, I think that it's pretty much a miracle that any of us survives.'

'What do you mean?' said the priest.

'I mean,' continued Andy, 'there's this one moment as you're growing up when the world suddenly feels more or less pointless – when the terribleness of reality lands on you, like something falling from the sky.'

'Something falling? Like what?' asked Father Frank, trying his best.

'Something big, like a piano, say, or a fridge. And when that happens, there's no going back to the time when it hadn't landed on you.'

'But what about the pleasure and the joy and the purpose, like sport, music, girls and the like?' Father Frank was nearly pleading now.

'Fiction,' sighed Andy. 'Mirages in the desert of life, to make people feel like it might be worth it.'

'Oh,' said Father Frank. 'Oh I see, and do all you youngsters get this feeling?'

'Yes, I think so,' said Andy, not even asking anyone else for their opinion, 'but most of us learn to live with it.'

'Well that's a relief, I suppose.'

It took me ages to find Stevie, who was sitting close to the church entrance in his wheelchair. His dad was nearby, fully occupied with the sober, repetitive job of shaking hundreds of hands.

'Oh Stevie,' I said and I leaned over to hug him and I closed my eyes and the tears that I'd been trying to keep inside came tumbling out.

'It's OK, Meg,' he whispered, even though obviously it wasn't. But I felt something a little like relief when I got a chance to look at his face properly. 'When did you get back?' he asked, and I told him we'd been back since the night before. That we'd come as quickly as we could, as soon as we'd heard the news. It occurred to me that part of the reason everything felt so wobbly was because I must still be jet-lagged. I couldn't see straight.

But surrounded by this fog of grief mumbles, there was a gladness in Stevie, a light in his eyes that lifted my heart slightly, and made me feel that maybe there was some reason to be cheerful, or hopeful, or even faintly optimistic.

'What happened, Stevie? What on earth happened? And why is everyone acting like this? This mass? A *mass*? I mean, you're not supposed to do that unless it's completely clear that the person you're having it for is definitely dead. Not unless there's proof. I mean, there's no reason for us to believe he's *dead*. Is there?'

Stevie looked up at me and swivelled a little closer.

'Exactly!' he whispered. 'That's what I've been trying to tell everyone! Thank goodness you're home Meg because seriously, you're the first person, the first person I've talked to – apart from myself – who doesn't believe it. I knew I'd be able to count on you and I'm *so* completely glad you've come back, because basically I felt on my own here, kinda thought I was going mad to be honest. Everyone's going round saying he committed suicide. I mean seriously, right? That doesn't make any sense – it really doesn't.'

'Stevie, you've got to tell me everything you know. Every single thing that happened before he disappeared.'

'I'll do my best, Meg,' Stevie said. 'I've been going over everything again and again in my head. There's no time to talk now though,' and Stevie frowned and looked around, and he sounded much older and wiser than a kid his age usually sounds. 'Let's meet at the pier later on. I'll see you there. Leave it till about midnight, OK?'

'How are you going to get there on your own at that time of night, Stevie?'

'No problemo,' he said, in a definitely non-grieving tone, which kept giving me hope. 'A lot has happened since you've been gone. I'm practically self-sufficient!' He grinned so widely that he started to attract some unwanted attention, so he changed his expression to something more grave, and, speaking with the furtive confidence of a spy, he told me to mingle, to say nothing and to meet him later as instructed.

The crowd milled. Arms were put around people and there was a lot more crying. Off in the distance every so often I glimpsed the golden hair of Paloma Killealy, and everywhere within the murmuring crowd I seemed to hear her name spoken softly from person to person as if it were a poem. Paloma Killealy. Paloma Killealy. Paloma, Paloma Killealy.